# AFTER CAGE

## CUBS FOR RENT #7

CHARITY PARKERSON

Punk & Sissy

--Warning: This book is intended for readers over the age of 18.

# INTRODUCTION

## CAGE MIGHT BE DOWN, BUT HE'S NOT OUT, AND HUDSON BELONGS TO HIM.

After a horrific accident leaves Cage badly scarred, he withdraws from the world. In this day and age of computer technology, he doesn't need to leave his house to amass a fortune as one partner in a giant gaming company. Cage has no trouble doing almost everything he needs from his desk. Unfortunately, he still needs someone to handle the errands and events he can't. Thankfully, he can afford to hire the perfect guy.

Three years ago, Hudson signed a contract to belong exclusively to Cage. He runs his errands, stands in for him at events, and keeps him company. While to most, they might seem to have an odd relationship, Hudson has grown accustomed to Cage's eccentric ways. In fact, he can't imagine sharing his life with anyone else. Except Cage doesn't want to come out of the shadows to live a full life with Hudson, and it's a hell Hudson can no longer tolerate.

When Hudson meets someone new, Cage will have to make a choice. He can continue living in fear or reach for the person he loves the most. He needs to decide fast, because Hudson is done with this half-life.

# ONE

*THREE YEARS AGO...*

In seven seconds, Hudson would force himself to move. Sometimes, he had to set time limits on his panic attacks, or they would take over his life. He had been oddly fine with this major life decision before five minutes ago. Everyone sold their time. It was called having a job. No matter his actual job title, this was pretty much just a career as a companion. He would run errands, keep some guy company, and do as told. That was nothing. It would be like taking care of his great grandmother before she died. There was no difference at all.

Hudson gave himself a sharp nod. It was like he was a nurse. Just because an escort—who was possibly more of a sex worker—had told him about this position, that meant nothing. So what if he had been required to submit a picture of himself before being hired. People were judged on their looks in job interviews every day, whether it was admitted or not. Hudson took a sharp breath. So what if he couldn't date anyone else and he might have to have sex with this guy who was probably eighty. The alternative was much worse than any of those things. His seven seconds were up.

With a deep breath for strength, Hudson held his head high and moved up the front walk. The white stone house was beautiful and gothic. Everything about it called to Hudson's inner romantic. He wanted to rush home and read a historical romance novel just from looking at the place. Hudson had no home, he reminded himself. He needed this job. It took all his willpower not to stop and literally smell the roses. Pink rose bushes lined the outside of the house and sidewalk. As Hudson climbed the front steps, the door slowly swung open. There was no one there—just like in a horror movie. Hudson tried breathing steady. Before full-blown terror could set in, a voice sounded through an intercom slash camera combo on the door.

"Hey, Hudson. Come on in. I'm a little busy at

the moment, but if you turn left and head to the kitchen, your contract is sitting there. Please go over it at your leisure."

He smiled, since he wasn't sure if he was being watched. "Okay. Should I shut this door behind me?"

"Don't worry over it. I can control it from here."

There was a small part of Hudson that wanted to be weirded out, but a contract sounded promising, and the voice was smooth and sexy. The guy didn't sound old. Following the voice's instructions, Hudson easily found the kitchen. It looked like a farmhouse kitchen, even though the appliances were obviously new. There was a huge stone fireplace. It looked big enough to cook in. There were also a few other amenities he hadn't seen in real life before. There was a dumbwaiter and laundry chute. He hadn't known houses really had those things. Everything about the place was something out of a dream for Hudson. A sturdy-looking wood table sat in the center of the room—like a family gathered around it every night and said grace before eating a home-cooked meal. Hudson moved closer. A stack of papers sat waiting. After pulling out a chair, Hudson sat and read.

He wasn't a lawyer and he couldn't afford one,

but it was pretty layman. Hudson would be expected to run errands, attend certain events, and generally do any job asked of him. In exchange, Cage Abernathy would pay him five thousand a month, give him access to transportation, make sure he was adequately dressed for whatever gathering he was required to attend, and provide him with room and board. In truth, while Hudson pretended to read every word, he really just skimmed. There was nothing he wouldn't do for that much money plus a place to live. He was on his last dime, on his last night of his paid hotel stay, and starving. Hudson hoped since this contract was already typed out with his name on it and everything that all he had to do was sign. Homelessness averted. He couldn't afford to balk or negotiate.

A small round speaker on the counter lit blue, capturing Hudson's attention a half second before the sexy voice filled the air again. "Does everything look in order to you?"

Hudson drew a steady breath. His heart skipped a few beats as he realized there was no going back. "Yes. I'm fine with these terms."

"Great. There should be a pen around there somewhere. Don't be afraid to dig through the kitchen drawers and find one. After all, this is your home now too. Once you're signed on, just leave the paperwork there and head upstairs, please. I'll direct you to your room so you can start settling in."

Hudson didn't end up having to dig. A black pen sat waiting beside the speaker. Before he could change his mind, Hudson quickly signed. For a moment he stared at his name scrawled across the dotted line. It was official. He was now the property of one Cage Abernathy. Hudson prayed he didn't regret this.

# TWO

"I swear to fucking Christ, Cage."

A chuckle rang through the drone hovering overhead. "You'll figure this out, beautiful. I have faith in you."

Hudson eyed the backyard and all the tiny holes he had dug. He took a breath. The clue had said his birthday present was hidden where all treasures were buried and where cows swallow blades but don't die. That was the yard... right?

"Do you need another clue?"

Hudson's shoulders fell. He had never been good at scavenger hunts. "Yes."

Luckily, Cage didn't tease him for being too

dumb to figure this out. "All right. I smash scissors and paper covers me."

A loud huff escaped Hudson before he could stop it. "Oh my god, Cage. There are rocks everywhere in this yard. How am I supposed to know which one?"

"Okay, baby. I'll stop teasing. You don't seem like you're having fun."

Now Hudson felt like shit. Cage didn't get much joy out of life. Setting up games for Hudson was the highlight of his day. "Give me one more clue." Even Hudson heard the unhappiness in his voice, but he wasn't giving up yet. He could figure this out.

Cage's voice turned sultry. "All shiny and silver with a beautiful face, you look in me, and find your place."

What was shiny and silver outside? Normally, he would think that riddle meant a mirror, but he had no idea where all treasure was buried that was near a rock and mirror. They didn't have a mirror outside. Goddamn. It was hard being the dumb one in the house.

"Oh my god. I can't take it. Our driveway is full of rocks."

Hudson felt twice as bad. He had ruined Cage's

game. Without a word and with his shoulders heavy from defeat, Hudson circled the house with Cage's drone following him. As he turned the corner, he spotted a very shiny and silver Audi R8. Hudson's feet froze to the ground.

"Holy shit."

"Surprise," Cage cheered. "Happy twenty-first birthday, gorgeous."

Hudson was speechless. Cage always did too much. "Wow. I don't know what to say. This is gorgeous." He moved closer and peered through the window. It had a burgundy interior. Hudson's eyes stung. "This is way too expensive of a gift, Cage. I'm blown away."

"You should come inside and eat some cake before you take her out for a spin."

That brought Hudson up short. "There's cake?"

"Of course," Cage said, as if it should have been obvious. "What do you think I've been doing in here while you were out there digging up the yard? Now come inside and blow out your candle before it burns down the house."

Hudson rushed inside with the drone hovering behind him. It flew itself to its charging dock while Hudson headed for the kitchen. There was always a ridiculous moment of hope before Hudson entered any room that he would find Cage standing there. Instead, the room was always empty. This time was no different. A slice of cake with a single lit candle waited for him. As always, Hudson fought his disappointment over being alone.

His smile felt fake. "Oh, yum. Chocolate. I don't know how you always pull off so much without me catching you."

"Make a wish," Cage said, ignoring his claim.

Hudson moved to the table. After taking a seat, he closed his eyes and focused. With every ounce of his being, he wished he would open his eyes and find Cage standing there. Hudson blew out the candle. He opened his eyes and the room was still empty.

To hide his defeat, Hudson focused on removing the candle from the cake. "I can't believe you're making me eat cake by myself on my birthday." His loneliness was always worse on his birthday. It was like a day had been marked on the calendar that existed only to remind Hudson he was alone in the world.

"You're not by yourself. I have a piece too. We're eating together. Plus, Lynx will be here a little later. You'll have some company today."

Hudson flashed the camera on the table a smile. He knew Cage was watching. He was always watching. Somewhere in the house, the disembodied voice had a face. A body. Somewhere, there was another beating heart, hiding from Hudson. Hiding from the world, except for Lynx. He would see Lynx. Hudson shoved a bite of cake in his mouth to keep his tongue busy.

"You're captivating."

A genuine smile tugged at the corners of Hudson's mouth. Goddamn it. This was why he stayed. Hudson shook his head, fighting a chuckle. Cage always knew when Hudson was at his breaking point with not getting to see Cage.

Hudson licked his fork. "Does it turn you on when I stuff my face?"

Cage's voice turned sultry. "Everything you do turns me on. I didn't realize how much of a voyeur I am until you came to live with me."

Despite his best efforts, Hudson's body reacted. "You don't sound like you're enjoying your cake."

"I definitely am. You should take yours upstairs."

Once upon a time, the suggestion might have made Hudson blush. After three years, there wasn't much Hudson wouldn't do on camera with the slightest urging from Cage. After all, it had been three years and Cage hadn't changed the channel. In fact, he acted as if he would never get tired of watching Hudson. No one understood how empowering that was.

"I don't know. I'm pretty comfy right here and I have a gorgeous new car to test drive."

"What if I told you there's another present waiting on your bed?"

That gave Hudson pause. The car was already too much. "Is there another present on my bed?"

A wicked-sounding chuckle filled the air. "There's only one way to find out."

The way that Hudson quickly jumped to his feet probably made him look spoiled. That wasn't what had him flying upward and heading for the stairs. He had wished to see Cage today. Some crazy form of childish dreaming made him think he would find Cage sitting on his bed. It didn't matter that his brain tried telling his heart there was no way that was true. Hudson still scurried to see for himself with Cage's happy-sounding laughter following him through the house. His bedroom door stood open, proving someone had definitely been inside. Hudson cleared the door and his heart dropped. Cage wasn't there. A teddy bear wearing a VR headset sat waiting for him instead.

Hudson fell back in to being a tease to hide how discouraged he felt. He slowly crossed the room and used his most flirtatious voice. "Well, now. Who is this guy?"

A sexy rumble of laughter caressed Hudson's ears, letting Hudson know sexual pleasure would soon follow. "I built this guy for you. All you have to do is strip, put the VR headset over your eyes, and your dick in the bear. Then I can blow your mind."

"In the bear?" Hudson asked as he picked up the equipment.

"He's a very special bear. You'll need your lube for this one."

Hudson turned the bear over; his backside had a hole. He was heavy too—like he was more robot than stuffed animal. "You want me to fuck a stuffed animal?"

"Do as I say, Hudson. I promise you won't regret it. This guy was built just for us. He's part of a set. I have the other one. We're about to be together, baby. Get undressed."

He wanted to be together. Hudson couldn't deny that. He set the bear aside and stripped. He kept his best assets facing the camera. Hudson wanted Cage to enjoy the show. His cock was hard at the idea of Cage sitting somewhere, stroking his erection and watching Hudson. Maybe that made Hudson a bit perverted. He liked being watched and didn't care if Cage knew it.

The moment he was nude, Hudson found his lube and oiled his cock, putting on a good show. Hudson was the only person to ever touch his dick; he knew how to make himself come the hardest. He waited until he heard a slight catch in Cage's breathing before moving to the bed. Hudson made a showing of pushing his erection inside the toy. He whimpered as he did so, for Cage's audio pleasure.

Once he was settled inside, he slid on the headset. A new world fired to life before him. The sexiest man Hudson had ever seen was on his knees between Hudson's. A suction moved on his cock in time with the guy on the screen bobbing on his dick. Hudson couldn't look away. It looked so real. Felt so real.

The suction stopped. The stranger's green eyes focused on Hudson. His lips moved in time with Cage's voice. "Settle in, baby. Let me take care of you." He went back to sucking Hudson's dick. Hudson fell backward, sprawling across the bed. He kept one hand on the bear so it wouldn't fall to the floor. His hips moved, rolling upward, and seeking more. Even though he knew it wasn't real and Cage wasn't in the room with him, the moment felt real. The suction on his dick and the images flashing across his eyes were devastatingly true to life. It looked like his room. His bed. Everything was the same except what sucked him. His mind was a mess. It felt good. He wanted the orgasm just out his reach. This was better than jacking off. Hudson needed to come. His heart raced as pressure climbed his shaft. He strained to reach what the pretend mouth offered. He moaned and gasped, being the showman, even as he fought to come.

"You're so beautiful." Cage's voice sounded so breathless—like he was on the edge of orgasm too. The thought had Hudson panting so hard, he could barely breathe. Cage kept talking in that sexy turned-on voice. "Now you can picture me as beautiful too as I pleasure you."

"You are beautiful," Hudson ground out as he openly fucked the toy Cage had built for him. "Your heart makes you the most gorgeous man on the planet. Nothing else matters."

"I love you, Hudson." The words caressed Hudson's ears like Cage was right there with him.

Hudson wanted that. "Then come to me right

now. I'll leave the VR goggles in place. I won't be able to see you. Come touch me for real, Cage. If you love me, come push your way inside me. I want to feel your dick stretching me wide and pounding inside me." Hudson didn't care he was begging. He was so close, and Hudson needed Cage to really be there just one time.

The suction on his cock sped and tightened. "Come," Cage ordered, making Hudson see stars.

Hudson's body knew its owner. The ability to breathe left him as the pressure climbing his cock exploded into waves of soul-rocking ecstasy. As his orgasm struck, Hudson's arms automatically sought Cage. They met empty air. The disappointment was real. It was a hollow punch to the gut even as his cock pumped cum into the new toy Cage had made for him. Cage groaned, reminding Hudson he wasn't completely alone.

Hudson clung to what he had of Cage, because— no matter what—he loved Cage. "That's it, sexy. Give me your cum. I want it."

Cage gasped for air. "Damn, baby. I wish I could taste your lips. You deserve kisses."

Hudson fought the urge to scream he was right here. He wanted those kisses. Instead, Hudson went with a different truth. "I love you, baby. You make me so proud, knowing I have your heart. The world should be jealous." Maybe their relationship was different. Perhaps, they lived a half-life, but Hudson loved Cage. At the end of the day, that was all that mattered.

---

WHILE HUDSON SHOWERED, CAGE RAN FULL speed on the treadmill. Hudson's pleas still rang in his ears. How much longer would his angel tolerate this? Fuck. Every day, Cage woke up determined to be a man. He could step outside this room. Hell, when Hudson was otherwise occupied, Cage had gotten damn good at moving outside his comfort zone to leave surprises for his baby and add more tech to the house so he could be everywhere Hudson was at any given time. Cage couldn't live without Hudson. Hudson was his eyes to the outside world, his connection to another soul, and Cage's heart. He was sickeningly in love with the sassy boy. A smile tugged at the corners of Cage's mouth. There was such a wickedness in Hudson's voice. He always spoke like he wanted to tempt Cage and be punished for it. Before Hudson, Cage had never been more turned on by anyone. Cage never got tired of him. He wanted to give Hudson the world.

"I didn't see Hudson when I came in."

Cage nearly jumped out of his skin. His heart raced into his throat. He stopped the treadmill and grabbed his chest, trying to keep the organ from bursting from his body. No one ever got the drop on him. Cage had been so distracted by thoughts of Hudson, he hadn't known Lynx was there.

"Goddamn it, Lynx. You scared the shit out of me."

"I announced myself as I came inside. The last thing I want is to ever catch you with your dick out while seducing Hudson with that VR game we made. Did he like it, by the way?"

An out-of-control smile pulled at Cage's lips. Only the fact that Lynx was his oldest friend and had been at his side before, during, and after the worst experience of his life allowed Lynx to be here now. Plus, without Lynx, Cage would probably be dead. Lynx knew everything. They had no secrets.

"He seemed to enjoy it, yes."

"Good," Lynx said, moving closer and plopping down in his usual chair. "Sex sells and I like money."

"You like driving your father crazy by getting richer and further out of his reach every day."

"Is that not what I said?" The heavy laughter in Lynx's voice made Cage smile.

"I finished coding the new section on Colt's game, if you'd like to try to convince Hudson to play when he gets out of the shower so you can test it out."

"You know I love hearing Hudson's bitchy feedback." Lynx paused for a second. "Speaking of the twink devil, he just stepped out of the shower. Wow." The hint of breathlessness in Lynx's voice couldn't be missed. Lynx cleared his throat, as if he realized how he sounded. "He really is beautiful. Just soft pale skin, big blue doe eyes, and thick curly dark hair. I can totally understand your obsession."

Cage's uncontrollable smile turned into a laugh. If anyone other than Lynx said those things, Cage would be jealous as hell, but it was Lynx. Despite his praise, Hudson wasn't his type at all. "I'm not sure 'obsession' is a strong enough word," Cage said, being honest. He had lost any sense of pride when he nearly lost his life. Plus, Cage wasn't ashamed of his feelings for Hudson. "He's pretty amazing. Anyone else would've left me a long time ago."

Lynx let out a loud and long mock gasp. "I'm still here."

Cage snagged his plush computer chair and sat.

"You don't count. Not only are you my best friend, we're business partners. That means you're stuck with me through a bond stronger than wedding vows. Hudson..." Cage stared at nothing, seeing nothing, as his thoughts gathered. "... he has an entire world of options, but he stays." Cage dropped his chin. "You're more in my life than he'll ever be, yet he stays."

"Yeah," Lynx said, sounding impressed. "He's pretty dumb."

Cage toed off his shoes and peeled off his sweaty socks. With a growl, he tossed them in Lynx's direction. "Get lost, loser. I need a shower."

"Ewww," Lynx squealed as he scrambled for the door. "You definitely do. I'll just go flirt with your hottie." The wickedness in his voice couldn't be missed.

Cage shrugged. "Go for it. You'll never be me."

"I know, gorgeous," Lynx said as he slipped from the room.

As the door clicked shut, Cage shook his head and stood. Only Lynx would still call him gorgeous. Without an ounce of conceit, Cage recognized he used to be. Years ago, he had been tall, blond, blue-eyed, and all smiles. Now he was just tall. Well, he supposed he was still blond too, but whatever. His hair could be any color. No one would ever see it.

Cage flipped the switch on the intercom and turned up the volume so he could listen to Lynx and Hudson while he showered. Their voices filled the large open area where Cage spent all his time. This floor of the house had everything he needed. A bed, all his office equipment, workout area, a bathroom, and even a fridge and tiny microwave. He never needed to leave.

Cage fired his shower to life. While he stripped, his mind drifted back to the days when he hadn't lived in fear and pain. Even though he hadn't been bad-looking, he had been a nerd. He still was, but now it didn't matter. Back then, in high school, when being popular was the most important thing, being a geek was just one more strike against him. Being gay was the ultimate black mark. In his senior year, when Cage met Miller, he had been on cloud nine every day and on his back every night. He hadn't realized how many bigoted sensibilities he had offended by falling so hard in love with a boy. Until six guys from his high school football team had held Cage down, doused him in gasoline, and set him on fire. That had changed a lot for him.

While he had survived, sort of, he had moved

away from that awful place and withdrawn from the world. Lynx tagged along and kept him grounded while he healed, and they worked together on starting Caged Lynx Games. Lynx brought the tech talent while Cage funded their venture with the money he had won through lawsuits against the boys' families. Between countless surgeries and coding for their new company, Cage had regained a lot, but not enough. The last he had heard, Miller was a cop now, back in Cage's hometown of Vegas. Miller had married a woman and had kids. It was odd knowing he had lost everything just to be someone's phase, but whatever. Cage had Hudson now. He couldn't imagine Hudson ever leaving him to marry a woman and have a bunch of kids. Cage was a big enough kid with all the best toys to keep Hudson entertained.

"Did you see my gift in the driveway?"

Cage froze with one foot in the shower as Hudson's voice washed over him.

"I did," Lynx said, using the teasing tone he always reserved for Hudson. "It suits you. Would you like a gift from me too?"

Hudson's adorable laughter filled the bathroom. With his eyes closed, Cage pressed his forehead to the shower wall. He couldn't stop smiling. No one knew how much he loved that sound. Everything had been so empty before Hudson's laughter filled the darkness. "Did you buy me a gift or are you asking if I want one? With you, there's no telling."

"Oh, I definitely didn't get you a gift. You're already too spoiled as it is. Ow! And you hit and you're just mean. I would've put you out a long time ago."

Cage chuckled at their antics. All happiness had gone from Cage's life the night of his attack. Then Hudson had signed their contract. He couldn't go back to the horrible existence he had lived before Hudson. Cage knew Lynx didn't completely understand. Sometimes, there was a certain disapproving tone behind his words when he talked about Hudson. Cage didn't know if it was the fact that Cage paid Hudson to be there or the idea of Cage refusing to show himself to Hudson that bothered Lynx. Hell, maybe Lynx didn't really like Hudson for some reason he kept to himself. Whatever unspoken thing it was, Cage couldn't care about Lynx's opinion on this. Cage was just a thing now. He was a useless, scarred monster with nothing to offer a man. But, for whatever reason, Hudson stayed. Cage would keep spoiling him and clinging to him, until Hudson had nothing left to give Cage. He doubted that meant Hudson would give him forever, but Cage had to try. When the day came that Hudson couldn't do this anymore, maybe Cage would give up too. He was very tired after all. Lynx would gain full control of the company and the world would never even know Cage was gone. No big loss at all.

# THREE

HIS NEW CAR was totally awesome. A car was still too much as far as birthday gifts went. Hudson felt guilty for accepting it. Still, he had to admit it drove like a dream. For the past three years, he had always driven Cage's SUV whenever he needed to go anywhere. The fifteen-year-old Lincoln Navigator was still in pristine condition and needed a driver since Cage never left the house. Hudson didn't really need a car, but wow. Cage always blew him away with his gifts.

Lynx hadn't approved. Cage's oldest and best friend hadn't actually said as much, but he didn't need to say anything. Lynx thought Hudson was a gold digger. Hudson tolerated Lynx's open disapproval of him because every job had one downfall and Cage loved Lynx. In all honesty, Hudson didn't dislike Lynx, even though Lynx didn't like him. Lynx was hard to hate. He was tall, skinny, and of Asian descent. Hudson suspected there was another race mixed in because he had the greenest eyes Hudson had ever seen. He was pretty gorgeous, even though he also had a short multi-colored Mohawk and never wore anything that was less than twenty years old. All his clothes had tears and holes. Iffy stains and god knew what else. But Lynx was funny and just overall likable. It was too bad he didn't care for Hudson. Sometimes, Hudson thought it might be nice to have a friend, especially one as loyal as Lynx was to Cage. Truthfully, Hudson was lonely.

The huge white home where the Kodiak brothers lived and ran their business, Cubs for Rent, came into view. He had only met the brothers on occasion. He had spoken to one of the identical triplets when he had signed on with their company. Hudson couldn't recall which brother it had been. They looked exactly the same, down to the finest detail. It was almost eerie. Other than that original meeting, Hudson couldn't recall a time when he had done more than nod at each one as he passed them at events. Hell, maybe he was nodding at the same

Kodiak all night each time he saw them. A chuckle escaped Hudson at the thought.

He found the valet and passed his new baby to a stranger. Hudson didn't want anyone else diving her so soon, but whatever. He never went anywhere anyway. With a deep breath for strength, Hudson climbed the front steps to the humongous home. Walking into events alone was the one thing that Hudson never grew accustomed to doing. While he was always alone—or never alone, depending upon how one looked at it—there was something about walking into a room filled with people that made him feel lonelier than never setting eyes on a single soul. Hudson felt exposed. It was like all eyes were upon him, judging him, and finding him lacking. They knew he didn't belong. He wasn't one of them. Hudson was a delivery boy, doing nothing more than gate crashing while waiting for the perfect moment to deliver Cage's donation to the proper person.

Expensive cologne and even more expensive people filled the ballroom. A waiter in a white uniform offered him champagne. Hudson smiled and shook his head. While he was twenty-one now, he was still driving, and Hudson was a lightweight. The crowd easily parted as Hudson headed for his usual spot on the fringes. He was a wallflower to his soul.

He usually cracked the French doors and enjoyed the night air until he could make his escape. Hudson also people watched. He liked making up stories about their lives to share with Cage. Hudson had always been a good storyteller. He assumed it came from his love of reading. However he had acquired the skill, it worked well for him keeping Cage entertained. For the most part, all they had was each other.

As his usual spot came into view, Hudson realized it was already taken. He almost moved along to find a different spot before the huge red-haired guy spun a cowboy hat between his hands in a nervous gesture. It dawned on Hudson that they had met. At the last event and in the same spot, the giant cowboy had shown up trying to win back his ex. He had been shot down in glorious fashion. Hudson felt a bit of kinship with someone being humiliated. He often felt that way for no reason at all.

Hudson crossed the room, pasting on his brightest smile. "Wow. A familiar face. That never happens to me. Is it okay if I join you?"

The man's unusual amber-colored gaze moved from Hudson to the empty seat beside him and back again. "Sure."

Hudson sat. He was pretty sure the guy's name

was Clint, but he couldn't be a hundred percent certain. Clint did not look thrilled to have his company. That was fair. Hudson didn't want to be there either.

"I saw you here two weeks ago, right?"

Hudson turned a bright smile his way. At least the guy was trying. That was more than anyone else would do tonight. He would know. No one ever talked to Hudson. "Yes. It's Clint, right? Or am I totally remembering that wrong?"

Clint's mouth lifted in one corner. He had harsh features—like he was hardened on the inside and it reshaped his exterior. "That's right. I don't think I caught your name."

"I'm Hudson," Hudson said, holding out his hand.

"You don't look like a Hudson."

The response took Hudson aback a bit as they shook hands. "What does a Hudson look like?"

"A balding middle-aged guy going through a mid-life crisis."

A loud laugh escaped Hudson at Clint's deadpan response. He covered his mouth, trying to smother the sound. "Maybe that'll be me in twenty years."

Clint eyed him, as if assessing the claim. "No.

You have a lot of hair. I doubt you'll lose it. Plus, you're the kind of guy who'll always look ten years younger than your age."

Hudson was oddly drawn in by Clint. He wanted to tease and laugh, making his hard edges smooth away with laughter. Hudson lowered his voice and leaned closer. "Holy shit. Are you saying I look like I'm eleven?"

Clint smiled.

Hudson's breath caught. He had known it would be spectacular.

Clint's huge chest expanded, and he shook his head, as if he didn't know what to make of Hudson. "What are you even doing here among this crowd?" Clint asked, surprising Hudson. "You look too sweet for this. Surely you're not selling yourself through Cubs for Rent."

"I am," Hudson said, straightening in his seat. He was somewhat offended by Clint's words. Nice people sold themselves all the time. The world wasn't kind to good people. "But then again, I'm not," he added, because honesty always won out. "I'm under an exclusive contract, so I'm not—technically —listed on their site, but I am considered an employee. But now I'm dying to know, what made you so certain I'm here as an employee and not a buyer?"

Clint looked uncomfortable, but he didn't back down. "You're too beautiful to be a buyer."

This one had too many wrong opinions, but Hudson wouldn't hold it against him. "Which are you?"

Clint's gaze continued scanning the crowd. He couldn't have looked more out of place. "Neither, I guess."

Hudson fought the urge to ask why he was there then. Instead, he chose a subject change. Couples were pairing off to dance. Hudson never got to do that. "Dance with me."

Clint's open discomfort doubled. "Um. I'm not really..."

It dawned on Hudson. While Clint was here, at an event meant for mostly gay men, he wasn't so out as everyone else there. Hudson had been disowned by his parents. Cage had been set on fire. Sometimes, being gay was terrifying. Hudson couldn't fault Clint for that. "Come on," Hudson said, coming to his feet and heading for the open French door. With one foot inside and one outside, he motioned for Clint to follow. "We'll dance out here. The music is every bit as clear, but no one will see us."

For a moment, Hudson expected to be shot down. But after a second passed, Clint stood and followed Hudson outside. Clint was huge. Not only had Hudson not danced since high school, Hudson had never danced with someone as tall as Clint. Luckily, slow dancing didn't take any skill. Clint set his cowboy hat on a metal patio table outside the door before moving closer to Hudson. Without a word, he snagged Hudson's waist, swept him into his arms, and spun. A loud squeal escaped Hudson as his feet left the ground. He wrapped his arms around Clint's neck and pressed his face to Clint's gigantic shoulder to smother the sound of his laughter.

A deep rumble of laughter vibrated from Clint's chest as he set Hudson's feet back on the ground. "I'm afraid I might break you if I manhandle you too much."

Clint's claim hit Hudson in the oddest way. He was the first person to touch Hudson at all in years. Hudson wondered if his skin would bruise in its shock. Still, he tried reassuring Clint. "I don't think I'll break that easily." For a few minutes, they moved together in time with the music in silence. Hudson soaked up the sensation of someone's body heat seeping into his skin. The backs of his eyes burned. It was ridiculous, but it had been so long. He could remember his great grandmother hugging him not long before she died, but he supposed that was the last time anyone had touched him. People didn't understand what it was like to go without human touch until it happened. That neglect did something to the brain. Changed him in some way. Made him smaller.

"Thank you," Clint said quietly, pulling Hudson from his growing despair. "I'm trying really hard to be who I want to be, but I'm not... brave, I guess."

Hudson smiled against Clint's chest. There wasn't an ounce of happiness in the gesture. "You have no reason to apologize. Life isn't always kind to anyone the least bit different."

Clint took an audible breath. "I haven't been kind either. I don't deserve your compassion."

Hudson had to force himself to move away from Clint's heat. He couldn't make himself lose the connection completely. While holding on to Clint's hand, Hudson headed for the table where Clint had left his hat. He sat and waited until Clint filled the chair beside him to speak. "This isn't compassion. I'm saving myself. These events are hell for me. I hate every second of these things."

Clint's brow furrowed. "Why do you come?"

"I'm standing in for my employer. He hasn't left

his house in years. Part of the reason he hired me is to come to these events in his stead."

"How did you end up doing this, if you don't mind me asking?"

Hudson shrugged. "I don't mind. Um." Hudson dragged out the word, trying to pick a place to start. Since he thought Clint needed to hear it, Hudson chose to start with what being open about his sexuality had done to his life. "Right after I turned fourteen, I asked my parents if I could invite my boyfriend to go to the movies with us. Honest to god, before that moment, I thought they knew I was gay. It's not like I tried to hide. I also never dreamed they would care. They'd never spoken badly of anyone in front of me. I'd never heard them use slurs or any such thing. They were my parents. I just assumed they would always love me no matter what. That was not the case in any form whatsoever. In the blink of an eye, my life was turned upside down. Before I knew what happened, I was living with my great-grandmother because she was the only family member who wouldn't let me live in the streets. For a long time, I was just in shock. Then the resentment set in. I kind of withdrew from everyone, which was just as well. My great-grandmother, Granny Fae, was already ninety. She held on until two months before I turned eighteen but then she was gone too."

When Hudson looked back on those days, he recognized he should have been terrified and in a panic. All he recalled was the deep shock and overall numbness. He shook his head. "She had changed her life insurance policy about a year before she died, making me the beneficiary. I imagine, if it had been any sum of money at all, my parents probably would've fought me for it. But it was only enough money to bury her and they didn't even show up for her funeral. I took the leftover money, which wasn't more than a few hundred dollars, and moved into a no-tell motel pay by-the-week type place. They didn't ask to see my ID or anything. Of course, once I met all the other people living there, I understood why."

"Drug addicts?"

Hudson shook his head. "Sex workers, and thank god for all those people. Without them, I never would've found my job with Cage. I was out of money and time. Without them, I probably would've been selling my body right alongside them, but they took pity on me and helped me find legitimate work. They said I was too soft for what they did." Hudson smiled at the memory. Those were the darkest days of his life, but the universe had sent him angels in his time of need. Angels who smelled like cigarettes and stale beer, but angels nonetheless.

"So, this guy you work for, is he like four hundred years old, or what?"

Hudson chuckled. Clint was like everyone when they learned about Cage and his hermit status. "No. He's thirty."

Clint blinked rapidly—like his brain misfired. "Okay."

Hudson's humor grew. "Is that it? Just okay? Most people have more questions."

Clint shrugged. "Without him, you probably would have ended up dead and then you wouldn't have been here tonight to save me."

Heat crept up Hudson's face. It had been years since he blushed. His gaze skirted toward the ground. He didn't know how to react. No one treated him like a savior.

"So," Clint said, dragging out the word. "You said earlier that you're in an exclusive contract with this guy. Does that count only for working or are you allowed to have friends?"

It was Hudson's turn to blink. No one had tried to be his friend in so long, he didn't know how to react. "I'm allowed to have friends."

"How about we have dinner tomorrow night, then?"

"As friends," Hudson reaffirmed, because he couldn't be clear enough on this point. Not only could Hudson not risk his job, he loved Cage. He wouldn't risk that for anyone.

"Right."

A smile tugged at Hudson's lips. He needed a friend and he had a feeling Clint needed one too. "That sounds great. Here," he dug his phone from his pocket. "let me get your number." They rattled off their numbers to each other and happiness grew inside Hudson's chest. It had been a really long time since he had something to look forward to. Something he wanted to do that was for only him. He hoped Cage was still awake when he got home. Hudson couldn't wait to tell him he had made a friend. Then maybe he could make Cage moan again. It was crazy how much he already missed the sound of Cage's voice.

---

THE ALARM BEEPED, LETTING CAGE KNOW Hudson was home. It beeped again as Hudson reset the system. Cage didn't bother getting out of bed.

Instead, he powered up the intercom system. He just wanted to hear Hudson's voice before his nightly meds carried him away. He snagged the wireless speaker and set it on the bed beside him. The sound of rustling clothes let him know Hudson made it to his room.

His bed creaked. "Hey, gorgeous. Are you still awake?" Hudson whispered the words, as if scared he would disturb Cage.

With his eyes closed, Cage pulled the speaker even closer. He wanted to feel the vibration of Hudson's voice. "Of course. Did you have fun? You stayed out later than usual."

"Meh. It wasn't as bad tonight. I made a friend, so I wasn't stuck sitting alone. Hey, did you know it wasn't a charity event tonight? I kept waiting around to make a donation on your behalf, but finally Toby explained it wasn't that type of gathering. It was some monthly thing they do to draw interest in their services."

Cage winced. "Yeah. I'm sorry about that, gorgeous. It's your birthday and I didn't want you sitting home. I knew you wouldn't go if you didn't think I was obligated. But you made a friend. Tell me more."

The bed creaked some more, as if Hudson settled

in beside his speaker. "I wouldn't have minded being at home tonight. This is my favorite part of the day, relaxing here with you, and listening to your voice. There's nothing I would rather do."

After rolling onto his side, Cage held his pillow a little tighter against his chest as warmth spread through him. "I love you."

"I love you too."

The emotion in Hudson's voice made it impossible to doubt him. That didn't mean Hudson had to give up living for him. "Just because I'm trapped here doesn't mean you should be too. Now tell me about your new friend."

"You're not trapped here, angel. Any time you want to step outside this house, I'll hold your hand. I would love that."

Cage's brow furrowed. "Are you avoiding my question for a reason?"

Hudson huffed. It was adorable. "I'm not avoiding your question. His name is Clint and he made money in racehorses and ranching. We hid from the party together. By the way, I think I'm going to take tomorrow night off."

That brought Cage up short. "Okay. You never take any time off, so I can't complain. Do you have big plans?"

"I don't take time off because this doesn't feel like a job to me. This is my home... with you."

Hudson always kept him smiling. "Do you know how sweet and beautiful you are?"

Cage swore he could hear Hudson blush. "I could say the same about you. You should come cuddle with me."

With his hand flattened against the speaker, Cage willed Hudson to feel him as strongly as Cage felt Hudson. "I'm already there. Don't you feel me?"

Hudson's voice immediately turned breathless. "I always feel you. You're in my chest everywhere I go. Whenever I say your name, I smile. You have no idea how much I never want to do anything else but be right here with you."

Cage's throat tightened. Hudson was a sickness for him. Cage wasn't strong. He hadn't been brave in many years. His life was fear and nightmares. Constant pain. The only bright spot in his life was Hudson. If he had to spend every dime he ever made to keep Hudson smiling, he would. Hudson was his most prized possession.

"Tell me what you're wearing."

A sexy chuckle made the speaker vibrate beneath his hand. Cage's heart sped at the sound. He could always tell when Hudson was about to get naughty. "Nothing. What are you wearing?"

A smile exploded across Cage's face. "One-piece pajamas with little footies and teddy bear ears."

"Perfect," Hudson said with a smile in his voice. "I've already fucked one teddy bear today."

A bark of laughter burst from Cage. Hudson was so much fun. He couldn't wait to see what he could convince the man to do next. Hudson was the perfect combination of sweet and dirty. Cage hadn't found a single thing Hudson wouldn't do for his entertainment. They had all night. Cage wasn't too tired for this and Hudson didn't sound like he was either. Maybe they could give that VR headset another go. He couldn't hear Hudson moan enough times to satisfy his heart. It was possible this was as real as they would ever be, but Cage didn't feel cheated. Their unique relationship was more than he had ever expected to have again. Cage wouldn't let Hudson regret choosing him. That wasn't an option.

# FOUR

"THERE'S an incoming text for Hudson from Clint."

Cage paused in the middle of coding their latest game as the words of the computer-generated home butler system, Charlie, filled the air. Hudson had given that guy his number. Cage bit back an aggravated growl. Keeping Hudson entertained in a public place was one thing. Texting Hudson was another. Cage didn't like that.

"What does it say?"

"I hope TJ Carrigan's is okay for dinner tonight. They only had an eight o'clock reservation available."

A shot of anger hit Cage in the gut. They had a contract. Hudson had made plans with another man, knowing damn well they were exclusive. It wasn't happening. "Charlie, generate a response to Clint from me. Clint, this is Cage Abernathy, Hudson's boss. As per the terms of Hudson's contract, he will not be meeting you tonight or any other night. I advise you not to contact him again if you do not wish to interfere with his employment status."

"Sending text now."

Cage nodded his satisfaction and went back to listening to Hudson sing along with the radio while he made lunch.

"Incoming text for Hudson from Clint."

Cage pinched the spot between his eyes. "Read it."

"Your boss just texted me and cancelled our plans. Is everything okay?"

The singing stopped. The silence that followed was deafening before Hudson broke. "What the fuck, Cage? Are you intercepting my texts? And did you cancel my dinner plans?"

Cage didn't experience an iota of guilt. "Yes, I did. You're under contract, angel."

Hudson growled. Cage smiled at the sound. The radio fell silent. Hudson did not. "You had better be fucking with me, Cage. It wasn't a romantic thing. It was only dinner with a friend."

"That guy doesn't want to be friends, gorgeous. You're just too nice for your own good."

"Not everyone finds me desirable, Cage."

Cage snorted. Yes they did. Even though he would never say as much, Cage strongly suspected that was why Lynx acted the way he did around Hudson. Lynx liked him a little too much.

Hudson wasn't ready to stop arguing. "You should know by now that you're the only—ow, goddamn it!"

Cage froze at the yelled curse. "What happened? What's wrong?"

Hudson whimpered. When he responded, he sounded strained. "I lost my temper and got distracted because you're being an overbearing ass. That's what happened. I was cutting an avocado for your stupid disgusting guacamole and sliced through my hand."

Cage came to his feet. He didn't know what to do. Hudson was hurt. Cage was trapped. "How bad is it? Do you need to go to the hospital?" The sound of Cage's racing heart filled his ears. He was useless in an emergency. Hudson needed him and he was helpless. "Talk to me, baby. How bad is it?"

The sound of splashing water and Hudson's

whimpers was the only response. Cage practically danced in place in his panic.

"I'll call Lynx. He can take you to the hospital."

"Don't fucking bother," Hudson snapped. "God forbid that be misconstrued as a date too. What then? Your best friend won't be able to come over anymore."

"It's not the same and you know it," Cage snapped in his panic and irritation.

"For fuck's sake. This really won't stop bleeding, Cage. It's really deep. I'm sorry. There's blood all over the kitchen. Your guacamole is ruined."

"Why are you apologizing? Fuck all that, Hudson. Let me call Lynx."

"I don't want you to call Lynx." Damn. Hudson was really mad at him. "I don't want your help. Just let me get it wrapped up so I don't bleed all over someone's car, and I'll hire an Uber. I'm sorry, but I doubt I can request a woman driver, so you don't misunderstand my emergency room visit as a date."

"Stop it, Hudson," Cage snapped, completely losing his temper. "You're being ridiculous and you're the one who had a fucking date planned with someone else. It takes an ass-ton of nerve to be mad at me when you're the cheat in this equation."

"Cheat? Did you just call me a cheat? You can go

fuck yourself, Cage Abernathy. I'm in here, cutting my goddamn hand off to make you food I don't even like, and I'm a cheat? Well, that's just beautiful." He said something else, but the sound of the front door slamming cut off his tirade and Cage's ability to hear him.

Cage fought back a panic attack. Hudson was hurt and he had left angry. What would he do if Hudson didn't come back? What if Hudson called this other guy for help? Cage hated being helpless. He snatched up his phone and called Lynx.

"*Hola*, sexy. How is my oldest and hottest friend today?"

Cage ignored Lynx's normal ridiculousness. "Hudson is hurt." Even he heard the overly loud panic in his voice.

"What happened? What do you need?" Lynx always came through for him.

"He cut himself pretty badly and he just left for the hospital alone."

Lynx hissed. "It's okay, babe. I'm getting my keys now. Don't worry. I'll meet him there and take care of everything. You know you can trust me to make sure your man is fine."

Cage took a calming breath. Lynx would take

care of Hudson. "Fair warning. I pissed him off, so you may not receive a warm welcome."

An irritated sigh rang through the line. "All right. Heading to my car now. Do you want to tell me what you did to upset him?"

Lynx already acted as if he didn't like Hudson. Cage didn't want to give him any ammunition against Hudson by saying Hudson had a date with someone else. "Not really. I just wanted to warn you he's pretty angry." Cage ignored the tiny voice in the back of his mind whispering he wasn't innocent in their argument.

"Okay. I'm on my way there."

Cage blew out a breath. "Keep me posted."

"Will do."

As Cage disconnected their call, he sat—hard—and stared at nothing. He ran through everything that happened in the last few minutes. One second, it had been a normal day. The next, everything was shit.

"Charlie, locate Hudson's phone."

"It's in the kitchen."

Cage leaned forward and lightly banged his forehead on the desk. He couldn't even text Hudson and try to make things better. Now that the heat of the moment had passed, he wasn't so sure Hudson had done anything wrong. Just because this guy had plans with Hudson, that didn't mean Hudson considered it a date. Hudson was so nice. He didn't realize how he made men crave. Goddamn it. Cage had called him a cheat. He'd ask what in the hell was wrong with himself, but Cage already knew what his problem was—he was in love with Hudson. Those weren't just words he occasionally threw the man's way. Despite Hudson always saying those words back to him, there was no way in hell Hudson could possibly love him for real. No matter what he said, it couldn't be true. There was nothing about Cage to love. What a nightmare the day had quickly become. Cage had no idea how to make it right.

---

WEARY AND HURTING, HUDSON LEFT THE ER with no idea how he would get home. He had been in a panic and angry when he left the house. After hiring his Uber through the app, he had walked away and forgotten his phone. He had been so angry with Cage, he couldn't think straight. Of course, it wasn't like he could use his phone one-handed anyhow. As he stepped out into the waiting room, Lynx shot to his feet. Hudson should have been relieved he didn't have to walk home, but he fought the urge to cry instead. He was already upset and in pain. Now he had to deal with Lynx's dislike and disapproval on top of everything else. No doubt, Cage had already told Lynx that Hudson was a cheat. A fresh wave of fury washed over Hudson at the thought. Never in a million years would Hudson have believed he wasn't allowed to have friends. Jesus. His life was a mess.

"Are you okay? What are they saying about your hand?"

Lynx's concern seemed genuine, which was odd. He shrugged, feeling exposed. "They don't think I severed any tendons, but it was pretty deep. It took twelve stitches to close it."

Lynx winced. "Do we need to run through the pharmacy drive thru and pick up any meds?"

"If you don't mind." Hudson winced as he said the words. He hated everything about this. The last thing he wanted was to be dependent on someone who hated him, but he needed help.

Lynx nodded. "I'll take care of everything."

Tears welled in Hudson's eyes and he quickly looked away. "Thank you." His voice broke and gave out halfway through the words.

"Hudson." At the unhappiness in Lynx's voice,

Hudson's gaze slid back his way. "I..." He shook his head and motioned toward the door. "Let's go."

With a tired nod, Hudson headed for the parking lot. He kept his head down and didn't say a word unless he had no other choice while Lynx took him to get his meds before taking him home. As Lynx pulled into the driveway, his headlights swept across the garage door, making Hudson realize how late it had gotten. The whole day had already passed while he had been immersed in his misery with Cage's hateful words rattling around inside his head. He didn't know what to do.

Hudson held his bandaged hand against his body, trying to ignore the throbbing pain that shot through his palm with each heartbeat. He stared at the darkened gothic-style house he had loved from the first time he set eyes on it. Tonight, he hated it. It looked like a prison. He was so lonely while never being alone. He was in pain and he wanted his mom. His eyes stung at the thought. This was the first time he had really been hurt since his parents decided they didn't love him anymore. Hudson felt like a baby and wanted to be cared for, but it would never happen. He sniffed, fighting back tears again.

"Why do you stay?" Lynx's question startled Hudson, reminding him he was wasn't alone with his self-pity. Lynx continued, expounding on his question. "I mean, I love Cage. He's my best friend and I see that he does a lot for you. Hell, he's done a lot for me, but you're not me. You're the one who..." Lynx growled. "Fuck. Never mind. I don't know what I'm trying to say here."

Hudson was too heart weary and in too much pain to try to wade his way through Lynx's weirdness tonight. Hudson pushed open the car door. "Thank you for coming to get me. I know you did it for Cage, but I still really appreciate it."

For a moment, Lynx stared at Hudson in silence. "Damn. You're really dumb."

While Hudson was certain Lynx was trying to make a point and wasn't intentionally being mean, it was literally insult added to injury while Hudson was already at his breaking point. "Thanks for that." Hudson didn't wait to hear more. He jumped from the car. With the last of his strength, Hudson headed inside without looking back. He couldn't care less about anyone's feelings tonight. No one else cared about his.

"Oh my god, Hudson. Are you okay? What did the hospital say?"

Hudson ignored Cage's questions as he climbed the stairs to his bedroom. Maybe he was being childish, or maybe something inside him had finally broken. Lynx had pointedly asked why he stayed. That meant other people saw this arrangement as weird and pointless. It was one thing for Hudson to know his life with Cage wasn't normal. It was a whole other for other people to question things—like they whispered about them behind their backs.

Hudson was in a bad place tonight. He couldn't be who Cage needed right now. For once, he felt selfish. He realized he needed a human touch. It wasn't normal or natural to go his entire life without that interaction. In his time of need, when it mattered the most to his heart, there was no one there to hold him. Bitterness welled inside him, getting larger by the second. Hudson needed a break from Cage. So he closed his bedroom door, draped a shirt over the camera in his room, and unplugged the speaker while Cage begged for a response. Silence pressed on his eardrums as Hudson sat on the edge of his bed. For a moment, he stared at nothing, seeing nothing.

There was more than one hundred thousand dollars in his account. With room, board, and transportation provided for the last three years, Hudson hadn't spent much of his salary. Tomorrow, he would start looking for a new job and place to live.

Lynx was right. Why did he stay? Hudson would never love Cage hard enough to make the man secure enough to trust him. A tear dropped from his chin to his legs, making Hudson realize he was crying. He didn't know when the tears had begun. Hell, maybe he had been silently crying since that blade sliced through his skin. It was like the skin on his palm had been the fabric holding him together. The moment he cut himself, all his pain poured out.

Hudson curled onto his side on the bed. In a fetal position, he held himself, since no one else would do it. He made no attempt to wipe away the tears that freely flowed. Hudson cried for the parents that didn't want him and the man who also never would. He cried because he was weak and in pain. Hudson cried because he needed someone to take care of him for once and there was no one. He was alone. As the tears rolled from his eyes to the bed, Hudson embraced the pain. He vowed this would be the last time he cried for all the people who didn't want him. Tomorrow, he would be stronger.

---

Cage sat on the floor outside Hudson's bedroom and listened to him cry. His chest hurt.

Even though he knew there was only one way to fix things, he wasn't sure he was strong enough to do what needed to be done. In the past three years, Cage had come to depend on Hudson being there. He couldn't imagine his life without Hudson's teasing laughter. That had turned into a selfish sentiment at some point. He was making Hudson miserable. Cancelling that dinner with Clint was nothing more than Cage's insecurity rising to the surface. Never before had he tried to control Hudson. Unfortunately, it seemed it didn't take much of a heavy hand to break Hudson.

Cage pushed to his feet, leaving Hudson to his tears. He called Lynx as he made his way back to his room. Lynx answered right away, as if he had been waiting to hear from Cage since he dropped Hudson off at the house.

"Is he okay?" Lynx asked without bothering to say hello, and proving things were every bit as bad as Cage suspected.

"I don't think so. He's shut himself inside his room and unplugged the intercom system."

"Damn." Lynx's curse perfectly summed up Cage's feelings.

Cage took a breath for strength. Once the words were said, there would be no going back. For once,

Cage needed to put Hudson first. He never would as long as their contract stood. "I need one more favor from you, and then I won't ask for anything else ever again."

Lynx snorted. "We're friends. Taking care of each other is what we do."

Cage had a feeling he was about to test the bounds of that claim. But at the end of the day, Cage loved Hudson. Sometimes love meant letting someone go so they could find happiness. Cage wasn't strong enough to give Hudson a real life. If he didn't want to kill the thing he loved, Cage needed to stop suffocating Hudson with this half-life he had saddled Hudson with. Butterflies were so much more beautiful in an open field than pinned to a board. It was time to let Hudson fly away.

# FIVE

DEHYDRATION PULLED HUDSON FROM
SLEEP. His throat hurt, his eyes felt gritty, and
Hudson's hand throbbed so bad that Hudson gasped
as the first twinge hit. Everything hurt—like someone
had beaten him with a bat in his sleep. He rolled,
wincing against the sunlight. Cage hadn't let him
sleep this late in ages. Of course, Hudson had
disconnected his speaker, so unless Cage wanted to
leave his room, he had no way to wake Hudson. He
glanced toward the clock. A white legal-sized
envelope leaned against the clock, blocking the
numbers from sight.

Hudson's brow furrowed as he reached for it. He
hadn't heard anyone come in. It took a little work to

pry the letter from inside with only one hand. A short and to the point letter along with a check were the only things inside. The check was for thirty thousand. Six months' salary. Severance pay. He was to be out by the end of the day. If Hudson had ever tried picturing this moment, he would have imagined anger, tears, and shouting. Instead, Hudson felt nothing as he stared at the legal print that held not a hint of personalization. The same numbness he had experienced the day his parents packed his bags overcame Hudson now. He stood and headed to the bathroom. Hudson needed a shower before facing this day.

Showering turned out to be a task as he tried keeping his bandage and stitches dry. Dressing and packing his things was an even worse experience. It turned out to suck being one-handed. Thankfully, Hudson didn't have a ton of stuff, especially since he had no intention of taking anything Cage had bought him over the years. Every gift from Cage had been a lie. Each time Cage had given him anything, it hadn't been in the name of love, as he claimed. Apparently, there had been invisible strings to Cage's love. Or maybe Hudson was just completely disposable to everyone. As long as he stayed quiet and obedient, he could have a home. The moment he stepped over lines he didn't know existed, he was gone. Hudson would cry, but he was too empty. He had no tears left to give.

As Hudson strapped his two rolling bags together to make them easier to handle, Lynx stepped inside the room. "Hey, angel. How's the hand today?" He didn't even look Hudson's way as he asked the question. It was beyond obvious he knew Hudson had been put out. It dawned on Hudson that Lynx had likely been sent to ensure he left without stealing anything. Fantastic. He wasn't trusted in any way, apparently.

Hudson turned away and added the last of his toiletries to a smaller bag he could carry on his shoulder. Between it, a backpack, and the two rolling bags, Hudson could get everything he owned in one trip. "I'll live." Damn. His voice sounded like he had been eating glass.

"Oh. Okay. So Cage asked me to set you up in a new place today."

"I don't need Cage to find me a place." Even to Hudson's ears, he sounded dead—like all the life had been sucked right out of him.

Lynx cast a look around the room and rocked

back on his heels—like he was nervous and still didn't want to look directly at Hudson. "Really? Where you headed? Back to the parents?"

Hudson tossed a disbelieving look Lynx's way. "I take it Cage never told you how I ended up here."

As he shook his head, Lynx stared at the opposite wall. Hudson had never seen him look so uncomfortable. It was almost like he didn't relish the idea of being the one to see Hudson out. "You're hot, and I assume this pays good money. I kind of wish I was hot too. Selling myself would drive my dad into an early grave." He smiled, as if he relished the thought.

For a moment, Hudson stared at Lynx. There was so much stupid that fell from Lynx's lips in that one statement that Hudson didn't know where to start, but he was tired of being quiet. "Last night, you called me dumb."

"Yeah, I'm sorr—"

"You're the real dumbass," Hudson said, cutting him off. "You have parents who love you and can't be driven away no matter how hard you push, but you just keep pushing. All it took for my parents was learning I'm gay." Lynx was looking at him now, and all Hudson felt was tired. He grabbed his bags, ignoring the pain that shot from his hand all the way up his arm as he hit his cut. Hudson focused on Lynx one final time. "I didn't beg my parents to love me the way parents are supposed to love their kids, and I won't beg Cage to love me the way he said he did. So there's no need for you to look so uncomfortable. Be free, Lynx. I can find my own place to live. There's no need for you to pretend to like me anymore."

"Hudson, I—"

"Save it. I can't swallow another lie right now. I know exactly why you don't like me. Always have," Hudson said, walking away. It would be a long walk to the bus stop with all his worldly possessions in tow. With one injured hand making things harder, Hudson would need all his strength for the trip. Honestly, Hudson didn't know how much he had left to give, but he wouldn't waste it on Lynx.

CAGE KEPT HIS HEAD DOWN, RESTING HIS forehead against his crossed arms on his desk. He listened to every word exchanged between Lynx and Hudson. It was odd how much he learned about the people he cared about the most in that one conversation. Maybe he should have let Hudson unplug that intercom sooner so Cage could plug it back in on the sly to eavesdrop. He had learned a lot from not only Hudson's words but from his tone. Hudson was bitter and exhausted. Angry. His rage wasn't limited to Cage. It seemed Cage wasn't the only one who had noticed that underlying thing between Lynx and Hudson.

He knew the moment Lynx entered the room. Cage could pick out Lynx's over enthusiastic step in a crowd. He didn't bother lifting his head. "You called him dumb."

"Well, yeah," Lynx said without an ounce of guilt tinting his voice. "For three years, he's lived right down the hall. At any time, he could've stormed this room and demanded you live again for him. Honestly, I think he's the only person who could force your hand. But he never tried. Only someone completely dumb and blind wouldn't have seen how far you would go for him. Now he's gone." Lynx fell silent for a moment, as if distracted mid-speech. A growl rent the air. "And the stupid, stubborn motherfucker just walked right by the brand-new car you bought him and down the street, carrying all his worldly possessions with a stitched-up hand. I hope you're both happy now. Dumbasses."

Cage sat up and scrubbed at his face. He wanted to scream and rage against the unfairness of life. But

Cage had done all those things years ago, and it changed nothing. Now, he was just tired of getting up every day when there was zero point to anything. Cage sounded weary even to his ears when he spoke. "I know you don't want to, and he probably won't let you help, but would you go after him, please? If he won't take the car I bought him, maybe he'll at least let you drop him off somewhere."

"You're a complete idiot," Lynx said, sounding truly angry for the first time. "Beg him to come back. Step outside and reclaim the man who fell in love with you even when you gave him no real reason to do so. What's the worst that could happen? You've already lost him. Take a goddamn chance, Cage."

Cage rubbed his temples. His head was on the verge of explosion. "Please hurry, Lynx."

"You know what." Lynx was angrier than Cage had ever seen him. His voice shook with it. "I'll go and I'll try to convince Hudson to accept my help, but I'm not doing it for you."

"I know."

He wondered if Lynx would burst a blood vessel in his anger. "How can you just sit there? You said you loved this guy. How can you do nothing right now?"

"Because I love him enough to set him free from

the burden of me. Please don't let him hitchhike or whatever he plans." Even to Cage's ears, his voice sounded dead. That was because he was. Maybe his body was still moving, and words still escaped, but he no longer had a heart. Cage imagined he would fall over any second.

After another irritated huff, Lynx stormed off, leaving Cage to wallow. Lynx didn't understand. No one did. Cage was nothing now. He had no right to steal Hudson's time and affection. It was best for Hudson to go now, so he could stop crying. Cage loved him enough to want him happy above all else. Hudson would never find happiness here.

---

THE SHELL AROUND HUDSON'S HEART THAT WAS keeping him safe was cracking. He shored it up with anger. Hudson ran through the list of things he had given up for Cage. Privacy, for one damn thing. He had been watched, listened to, and had his texts read all hours of the day. Not that Hudson talked to anyone, but still. Who did that? Crazy people, that's who. He had lived the last three years as an eccentric man's twenty-four/seven reality show or like a fish in an aquarium. Whichever choice exposed him the most, that was him. Then, the first time he didn't obey, he was out. Well, fuck that. Fuck everything about that. He was done. Oh, and then, Cage had sent the friend that hated him to find him another place to live. They both could kiss his ass. Hudson was finished dancing for an audience. Cage and Lynx could have each other. One of these days, Cage would realize it was really Lynx he wanted anyhow. It was best if Hudson got out of the way. Bastards.

"Get in the car, Hudson."

Hudson's head whipped around to find Lynx slowly driving beside him. "You look dumb as hell right now," Hudson said, because he couldn't stop dishing out the same insult Lynx had thrown his way last night. "You look like a man begging his wife to get back in the car after an argument."

"Or maybe you're the one who looks ridiculous, walking down the road with everything you own, and refusing help," Lynx shot back.

He had a point. Hudson stopped to glare at Lynx. "Why do you care, Lynx? You finally got rid of me. You have your way. Go back to Cage. You no longer have to concern yourself that I'm robbing him blind of everything, including his love for you."

Lynx looked away and stared straight ahead while tapping his fingers on the steering wheel. He chewed his bottom lip for a second before meeting Hudson's stare again. "You're right. When I first realized that Cage was falling for you, I didn't like it. He spent a lot of money buying you gifts and keeping you entertained. I thought you were taking advantage of a vulnerable and lonely man. But then, he stopped hiring a cleaning service because you took care of his home. He stopped paying for food delivery and laundry services. One expense right after the other disappeared because you did everything to make his life easier. Eventually, I had to admit you did those things because you care. I know you love him, and I know this anger right now is because you're hurting. Let me help, okay? At least let me drop you off somewhere."

Hudson's hand hurt. That was the excuse Hudson gave himself to accept. He opened the back door and shoved his bags inside before climbing into the passenger seat. "Just take me to the closest hotel. I don't care which one. Please and thank you." He never looked Lynx's way.

Lynx pulled away from the curb. "For the record, I'm sorry this happened. I think you'll both be less for this loss."

"Just make sure he eats." Hudson stared out the passenger side window as he said the words. Lynx would take care of Cage. Hudson didn't need to worry about that. They had been looking after each other long before Hudson had come along. Worrying about Cage was pointless. He didn't need Hudson at all. No one did.

# SIX

HUDSON: *This is Hudson. I have a new number. Sorry in advance for writing a book-long text, but I'm one of those who says everything in one message, lol. I'm sorry about not texting you back the other day. After I got your message, all hell broke loose, and I ended up in the hospital. Nothing serious. Just a cut that needed stitches but that led to some other crap and you got lost in the fray. Sorry again. Anyhow, I'm settling into a new place and I would love to finally have that dinner. I'm a pretty decent cook. How do you feel about coming over?*

Clint: *Did I get you fired?*

Hudson: *No. Don't think that. I lost my temper, and apparently, I wasn't allowed to do that. So I'm*

*unemployed now. No big deal. So... about that meal?*
*\*hopeful face\**

Clint: *Yeah. I'd love that. I'm out and about now.*
*Do you need me to pick up anything on the way?*

Hudson: *Nope. Just bring yourself.*

Clint: *I can only stay a couple of hours, because I*
*have an appointment later, but I'm on my way.*

---

EVEN THOUGH IT WAS RIDICULOUS, HUDSON WAS nervous about Clint coming to dinner. He couldn't explain it. Things had been such shit lately that he half expected something horrible to happen. He had gotten a new phone and then shipped the one Cage had given him back to Cage. It felt like he hadn't had a moment to relax since his life fell apart. Now that he was a little bit settled in at a short-term rental, he wanted to move on with his life and keep the one friend he had made. The moment Hudson sat with Clint at the kitchen table with food between them, Hudson's discomfort fell away. They were friends. That same connection he had felt with Clint on his birthday was still there. They still had that same kinship.

"Where did you learn to cook? This is amazing."

A smile tugged at Hudson's lips. He didn't have much of an appetite, but Clint seemed to be enjoying his pork chop dinner. "I lived with my great grandmother as a teenager. She no longer had the strength or stamina to cook big meals, but she could sit at the kitchen table and direct. She taught me everything she knew."

Clint nodded. "My mom tried to teach me how to cook when I was young. But anytime she tried to do anything that Dad considered the least bit feminine, he would put a stop to it. To him, men worked the land. Women were in the kitchen. The barefoot and pregnant mentality. He was a horrible bastard. Always angry for no reason at all." He looked thoughtful for a moment. "I suppose I turned out to be just like him."

Hudson liked Clint. He was hard, but he knew it and tried to be different. "They say it's inevitable for everyone to become their parents. I hope that's not true. Mine are terrible people."

A deep rumble of laughter escaped Clint. "That's probably not even a possibility for you." Before Hudson could decide if that was a compliment, Clint moved on. "Have you decided what'll you do now for employment?"

Hudson shrugged as he picked at his food. "I have a little time to think about it. Being a live-in employee afforded me the opportunity to save quite a bit of money. So, I don't have to rush. If push comes to shove, I could always list myself on the Cubs for Rent site." He flashed Clint a smile, expecting a commiserating look. Instead, Clint didn't look thrilled.

He lifted one shoulder in a half shrug. "I would offer you an exclusive contract like you had with Cage, but I had a somewhat similar arrangement with someone once. It didn't go well. Someone like me shouldn't have that much power over anyone."

"What do you mean 'someone like you'?" Hudson had given up on eating in favor of staring at Clint. He looked sad. Hudson wanted his secrets.

Clint set his fork aside and pushed his plate away. He took a quick swig from his beer before focusing his full attention on Hudson. Clint looked harsh and serious. "If I have the power and control, I'll hide. I'll let you feel meaningless, so I don't have to feel different." Clint blinked as if physically closing away a part of himself before Hudson got a real glimpse at him. A small smile curved his lips. "But I don't want to be that person anymore, so this is better. I want to be better."

A chuckle escaped Hudson without thought.

Clint's eyebrows rose. "What?"

Hudson shook his head. "I was just thinking. In a roundabout way, we're both trying to break out, yet—when we're together—we still find a way to avoid the crowd."

A bright smile exploded across Clint's face. "Hey, I tried to take you out to dinner."

"I'm sorry about that." Hudson held up his hand, showing off his bandage. "The guy at the ER said it was so common for people to cut open their hands while slicing avocados that it has a name: avocado hand. He said they see at least four people a day with the same injury. Twelve stitches, believe it or not."

Clint's gaze moved from Hudson's hand to hold his stare. He looked hard again. "You should have called me. I would've taken care of you. Some things you shouldn't have to do alone."

Hudson kept his gaze locked on his hand to hide the way he craved not being alone. "There wasn't time to call anyone. It was bleeding pretty bad. I wish I had called, though." Heat crawled up Hudson's cheeks, but he didn't stop telling on himself. "As horrifying as it is to admit, I didn't handle it well. I was a bit of a baby afterward."

To Hudson's surprise, Clint gently took his Hudson's injured hand between his. He peeked beneath the bandage and inspected the wound, as if checking the doctor's work for mistakes. Seeming satisfied, he lightly tugged the bandage back in place before bringing Hudson's hand to his mouth. His lips brushed Hudson's palm. He kept a light hold on Hudson's wrist and stood.

"I'm sorry to eat and run, but I promised to take a look at some horses for an ex-client. Would you like to come along?"

Hudson flashed him an apologetic smile. "I would, but the painkillers they gave me make me tired." It wasn't a total lie. The painkillers did make him drowsy, but Hudson hadn't taken any tonight. He was just depressed and swinging wildly between wanting company and wanting to be alone.

Clint nodded. "You should get some rest. Heal. Walk me to the door and I'll leave you to it."

They were literally feet away from the door, but the sentiment made Hudson smile. He dutifully followed Clint to the door. "Thank you for coming over. I'll admit it's been quiet since I moved."

"Thank you for dinner. You're an amazing cook. Next time, I'll take you out, because I am not a good cook." Clint smiled as he made the confession. He really was a gorgeous man. No doubt, if he ever completely came out, someone would scoop him up in five seconds flat.

Hudson couldn't stop smiling at the thought. While Clint was hard and somewhat cold, he was also steady and strong. Hudson's smile slipped away. He was tired of being strong. "That sounds great," he said, trying to hide his downward spiral. "Hug me and I'll set you free."

Clint didn't hesitate to close his arms around Hudson the moment Hudson stepped inside his hold. Neither of them moved away. Hudson wondered if Clint desperately needed a friend too. He seemed equally as unwilling to give up the contact. Hudson made the first move to pull away. As he leaned back, Clint changed angles and his lips touched Hudson's. Hudson's breath caught. His first instinct was to push Clint away. They were just friends and that was all Hudson wanted but he had never been kissed by a man. He had been kissed by a teenager when he was a teenager and they were too young to go much further or have much skill. This was different in every way. Hudson's brain stopped working. Clint gently held the back of Hudson's head. He was completely in control. Hudson couldn't breathe. Clint's mouth opened over Hudson's bottom lip. Curiosity had Hudson tasting him in return.

The air changed. Clint's hand found Hudson's ass. He hauled him closer until there was no space between them. Their tongues met and brushed. There was nothing friendly about any of it. Clint's intentions were plain. Hudson's chest hurt. Cage was right. Clint didn't want to be friends. Before Hudson could panic, Clint gently brushed his lips across Hudson's one more time and pulled away. He looked turned on. His cheeks were flushed and his eyes hooded. Oddly, his features were even harsher than usual.

"I'll call you."

Hudson nodded, even though he wasn't sure he would answer when that call came. As he closed and locked the door behind Clint, the shaking hit. His knees gave out and Hudson found himself on his haunches and bent at the waist. He had let Clint kiss him. Hudson had kissed him back. Tears welled in his eyes. He covered his mouth, trying to stifle the cry that welled in his throat. That kiss was supposed to be Cage's. Cage didn't want him anymore, if he ever really had, Hudson reminded himself. The heartbreak was real. It was devastating. Every day, it got harder to breathe. He wasn't supposed to lose Cage. Yet, here he was—empty.

A knock sounded on the door, bringing Hudson back to his feet. He swiped at his eyes, desperately trying to hide the signs of crying. When he opened the door, he found Clint, looking every bit as wrecked as Hudson felt.

"I love someone else, but he doesn't love me." Hudson nearly started crying again at Clint's confession. Clint wasn't finished. "I shouldn't have kissed you. If you can forgive me, I really would like to be friends. I don't have any of those."

Hudson massaged his own arm, trying to comfort himself. He nodded. "I don't have anyone either." He swallowed, wishing the pain away. "Maybe Cage doesn't really love me, but I'm not ready to let go just yet."

Clint held his hand out for Hudson to shake. "Friends."

Hudson shook. "Friends."

Clint used the handshake to pull Hudson back into his arms. He hugged him tight, making Hudson tear up again. He needed this more than he cared to admit. One day, he might recover, but today wasn't that day. Tomorrow, he would try harder to move on. Hudson hoped he could keep that promise to himself. Right now, it didn't feel possible.

# SEVEN

THE LENGTHS CAGE went to locate Hudson would likely horrify anyone if he was forced to admit them. He didn't care. It had taken him less than forty-eight hours to regret his decision to let Hudson go. The sound of Hudson's tears had fucked with him. Now, after looking back on the time they were together, Cage realized a few important things. He should have gone to Hudson. Hudson was already hurting, crying, and likely done with him that night. What would it have mattered if Hudson had seen Cage? Lynx was right. They were already over. How much worse could it be? To Cage, there was no bigger hell than being without Hudson. He hadn't understood how quiet life would be. Honest to god, it was no longer worth living. The darkness was pitch black now. He couldn't do it any longer. Cage didn't want to spend another day without the other half of his heart. It was unbearable.

At first, he had simply paced, trying to squelch the madness. Then Hudson's phone had arrived. It was like that phone landing back in his hands had been reality slamming down on Cage's head. Hudson was done. He wouldn't come back, begging Cage to change his mind. Not that Cage had ever expected that to happen, but still. They were done. Cage had really and truly lost the other half of his soul. He couldn't go on without Hudson. Hell, he was pathetic to the point that he was almost willing to share Hudson if he would just come back. That thought alone made Cage want to cry. He had truly turned into a mess since his life had blown apart. It was like he had no sense left. There was one good thing about having no pride left—he gave no fucks how crazy he looked now. He just wanted Hudson back at any cost.

Cage sat in the backseat of the car he hired with a box on his lap and his heart in his throat. He hadn't been this terrified in a long time. Leaving his home had almost done him in mentally, but it was too late to go back now. The car came to a stop. Cage didn't move.

"Do you need any help?"

Cage ground his back teeth at the question. This was one of the many reasons he had stopped trying to go in public. People took one look at him and treated him like an invalid. He smiled. "No, thank you." Cage gathered his things and stepped from the car. He waited on the sidewalk until the car pulled away and he was alone to unpack his box. Cage hoped no one was watching from their windows and called the police. The last thing he wanted was to explain this insanity. He had to start somewhere in his quest to win Hudson, though. Hudson was the one. Cage couldn't let him go. He had to try.

---

THE TINY HOUSE WHERE HUDSON WAS STAYING was only a temporary fix. Since he didn't have any furniture and no job, getting a place of his own wasn't plausible yet. He had gone with one of those places where people rented out their vacation homes to strangers. The place was fully furnished, stocked, and could be rented up to a full month, buying Hudson some time to decide what to do with his life.

After he had lain awake all night the night before, thinking, Hudson had come to one huge realization—he could go anywhere. Hudson didn't have anything keeping him in Austin anymore. He had money and freedom. Hudson could go anywhere. Do anything. After that life-altering realization, he had spent the whole day sitting at the kitchen table and surfing the web, dreaming while trying to regain some excitement for life. There were some nice places for sale in the mountains of Tennessee. It was affordable and Hudson preferred the quiet. He had no intention of ever falling in love again, so there was no need to live anywhere with any sort of nightlife. Maybe he would just buy a tiny one-room cabin in the hills and live out his life in peace. No one said he had to rejoin society. He could disappear. The idea comforted him more than he ever dreamed.

A loud bang startled Hudson's heart nearly into his throat. His eyes slid toward the back door. The sound came again, bringing Hudson to his feet. He crept closer, hoping he didn't end up dead when some madman burst inside. He wasn't used to living alone or in a place with zero security. But Hudson refused to live in fear, so he opened the door.

A growl escaped him.

"Can we talk?"

Hudson took a breath. Rage rose inside him like a tidal wave. He was fucking furious that Cage would send him packing and then send a goddamn drone to find him. It hovered at exactly eye level.

"Hold on," he said, holding out a finger to the hovering robot. Hudson turned away. His gaze skirted the room. Anger had his heart beating in his ears. He snatched up a nearby broom and unleashed his wrath. No doubt he looked like a crazy person, but Hudson didn't give a shit. He was enraged. It beat at his temples and eardrums, drowning out all sound. All the pent-up words burst from him as he swung at the drone. "You said you loved me, you son of a bitch. You were supposed to be different. You were supposed to be my family now." He swung, taking the drone to the ground. Even when it smashed to the porch, he wasn't satisfied. Hudson attacked it as if he held a bat instead of a broom. He felt his stitches pull and tear. Hudson didn't care. The pain only drove him. His chest heaved as he stared down at the smashed equipment. All the fight drained from him every bit as quickly as it had hit. He didn't feel better. At some point, the broom had snapped in two. He would have to replace that.

Hudson tossed the broken pieces on top of what was left of the drone. He wanted to cry. His breath came out stuttered as he fought the tears pressing at the backs of his eyes. He had just destroyed any chance he had of talking to the only person he loved. His anger had gotten the best of him. Hudson rubbed his chest. Even though he knew Cage couldn't hear him now, he still said what hurt the most. "I guess you never really loved me after all. You're just like everyone else."

"Don't say that, angel."

Hudson's head whipped around so fast, he nearly hurt himself. Cage moved out of the shadows. It was almost funny. Even though he had never seen Cage, Hudson knew him immediately. He was tall and skinny. A hoodie covered his head, even though it was still eighty degrees at night. Sunglasses covered his eyes, even though it was dark. Although Hudson couldn't see much of his body or face, he could see the angry scars around his scruffy beard and down his neck.

"Cage." Hudson's voice cracked as he said Cage's name. Tears slid down his cheeks with no input from his brain. Even though it wasn't his fault, Hudson felt like the worst person on the planet for forcing

Cage from the safety of his home to see him. He was so shocked at the sight of Cage; it took Hudson a second to realize Cage used a white cane to navigate his surroundings. Shock rocked Hudson to his core. Cage was blind. How was that possible?

Cage's lips quirked. "Hey, beautiful."

Hudson could barely breathe. He had never suspected. There were cameras everywhere inside Cage's home. Cage had said so many things that made Hudson believe he could see him. Hudson had done so many things, thinking they were for Cage's viewing pleasure.

"Did you leave me alone out here?" Cage asked, sounding nervous when Hudson didn't respond to his greeting.

With a sniff, Hudson tried pulling his shit together. "I don't know how you would know if I'm beautiful."

Cage winced, making Hudson's guilt double. He didn't have any reason to feel bad. This was all on Cage. Logically, Hudson knew that, but apparently, he was fucked up to his core. He sniffed again as more tears fell. Hudson couldn't stop crying.

"Don't cry, gorgeous."

"Fuck you. Don't tell me what to do." Hudson's eyes fell closed. He didn't know how to stop being so goddamn angry. Something warm trickled down his fingers. He glanced down. Blood dripped onto the porch. A long and loud sigh escaped him. "I tore open my stitches. You can come in while I clean up my hand if you want. Just be careful of the smashed drone. I would sweep it up, but I broke the broom in two while destroying it."

Cage pressed his lips together, as if fighting a smile before clearing his throat. "Don't worry over me. I'm a technology wizard. This cane is a smart cane. It can get me anywhere."

Hudson stole another second of staring at him. No one knew how much Hudson loved the sight of his face. "Okay. Well, I'm bleeding everywhere, so..." Without another word, Hudson walked away and left Cage to follow.

"Do you need to go back to the hospital?"

Hudson shook his head before he realized what he had done. It would take some time for him to adjust to the fact that Cage couldn't see him. "No. I'll just super glue it or whatever. I don't have health insurance. Or a job," he added out of spite. Hudson didn't look to see Cage's reaction.

"You had an exclusive contract with me," Cage shot back, sounding every bit as bitter and hurt as Hudson felt.

Hudson's anger made him forget about his wound. He reversed course and slammed the back door behind Cage. Nothing good could come of the neighbors hearing them yelling. He might get kicked out. "You never said I wasn't allowed to have friends and I never would've agreed with those terms."

Cage snorted. "That guy wasn't interested in being your friend, Hudson."

An aggravated growl tore from Hudson's chest. Cage was set on fighting. "You don't know anything about him or it at all. You just decided I was a cheat with zero provocation."

"I don't have to know him because I know you. You're nice, flirtatious, gorgeous, and irresistible in every way. No one wants to just be your friend."

Hudson was still mad, but he didn't know what to say to that, especially since Cage wasn't totally wrong. Clint had kissed him. Everything hurt. He couldn't back down or let this go. Hudson had never done a thing to deserve Cage's mistrust. "You weren't there. You didn't see his face at that event. He was just lonely."

"And you're just you, sexy. Every man wants you, especially the lonely. Goddamn, I should know." Cage stopped, dropped his chin, and sucked in a deep breath as if determined to get his temper under control. He swiped back his hood. Blond hair spilled out as his hood fell away. Maybe Cage's face was heavily scarred, but he was beautiful to Hudson. Hudson's heart squeezing in his chest gave Cage time to reenergize to keep arguing, but his tone was calmer. "When you came home that night, I could hear it in your voice when you talked about him. You're the one who was lonely. Maybe this guy was too. I don't know. Like you said, I wasn't there. But you can say what you want, because we both know that dinner would not have ended as just friends."

Hudson turned away and headed for the sink. He tried not to think too hard as he wet a paper towel and tried cleaning away the blood without getting what was left of his stitches wet. It wasn't horrible. Only a small part of the cut had reopened. Without his permission, Hudson's mind went back to that night. That dance. The conversation they shared. Maybe Clint had looked at him with a little heat. Held Hudson a little too close. In retrospect, he should have realized Clint would make a move if given the chance, but Hudson could fill a thimble with what he understood about men, and none of that mattered anyhow. At the end of the day, Hudson loved Cage and he had gone home to Cage.

If Cage hadn't put him out, Hudson would have always chosen Cage.

"You're wrong," Hudson said, holding a dry paper towel against his cut and trying to stem the bleeding. He didn't look Cage's way. "It doesn't matter at all how Clint feels or if he wanted to be more than friends. Nothing matters. Not even my loneliness." Hudson wouldn't deny that part. He covered the cut with a Band-Aid and finally turned Cage's way. "The fact is, I love you. Nothing would've stopped me from always coming home to you. No one could convince me to choose them over you. It doesn't matter what other people feel about me. It only matters how I feel, and I only wanted you. You're the one who decided you didn't want me anymore. So what are you doing here now?"

"I miss you."

A huff escaped Hudson. "That's it? You miss me. For three years, I've been right down the hall and you couldn't step out the door. Now you toss me out and here you are. Your so-called love feels a hell of a lot like hate."

Cage dropped his chin. His chest expanded on a deep breath. "I shouldn't have called you a cheat. You didn't deserve that. I've never had to share you.

If this guy makes you happy, then I love you enough to accept that."

"For fuck's sake," Hudson said, throwing his arms into the air. "We are only friends. He's in love with someone else and I love you, for some dumbass reason. You've already kicked me to the curb, so what is this, Cage? Have you decided that you hate so much that you need to kick me some more? I'm not going to beg you to trust me, because I've never done a goddamn thing to deserve this treatment."

"I'm trying," Cage said, sounding pained. "I'm here. You know I wouldn't have stepped outside for anyone else."

Hudson was still mad as hell, but it was Cage. He had shown up and that was more than Hudson ever imagined. He didn't know whether to laugh or cry over his bar being set so damn low.

"Come on," Hudson said, sounding tired even to his ears as he crossed the room and took Cage's hand.

"I don't need your help."

Hudson's already frayed temper snapped again. "Maybe I just want to hold your hand, Cage. Goddamn. Did you ever think of that? Did it ever once occur to you that I might need to touch you? Why does everything always have to be about you?"

Cage's grip tightened on Hudson's hand. "Lead the way."

With an inner sigh of relief, Hudson headed for the living room. Cage's hand felt so warm against his. It was probably the satin gloves Cage wore in the middle of the summer, but Hudson also wasn't used to holding hands. When they reached the couch, Hudson urged Cage to sit, but he found he couldn't let go of Cage's hand. He filled the spot beside him, sitting much closer than necessary. Cage shifted, taking his hand back. Before Hudson could experience an ounce of disappointment, Cage draped his arm across Hudson's shoulders and held him close. Hudson's eyes fell closed. He moved his head until he could find Cage's heartbeat with his ear. Hudson lightly rubbed every place he could reach. Cage's stomach. His thigh. Hudson's eyes stung as he sucked in Cage's scent. He smelled like the home they had shared. That almost broke him.

"You're so tiny." The words vibrated against Hudson's ear. "Lynx is always describing you to me, but I don't think I realized exactly how small you are."

"You're hairier than I imagined."

Cage shook with laughter. "It's easy not to care

about haircuts and shaving when no one sees me, not even me."

Hudson swiped at his eyes. He had turned into a watering pot lately. It was like years of built-up pain couldn't stop pouring out. "I think you're gorgeous."

"Maybe I'm not the only blind one." Even though there was heavy laughter in Cage's voice, Hudson still pulled a face. He didn't like Cage thinking badly of himself.

"Maybe I'm the only one of us who can see, so you should believe me... for once."

For a moment, Cage fell completely silent. Hudson swore he didn't as much as breathe. When he spoke, his voice was flat—like he expected the worst and braced for it. "Do you plan to ever forgive me?"

"Do you plan to apologize?" Hudson shot back.

Cage gave him a sharp nod. "One of these days."

A smile exploded across Hudson's face. He couldn't help it. As much as he was still tempted to punch Cage in the stomach, he also loved him so goddamn much, it hurt. "I'll look for your three-page summary on where you went wrong."

Cage smiled. It was sweet and melted Hudson's insides. Even while wearing sunglasses, he could see the way Cage's eyes crinkled. "Three-page summary, huh? That seems fair. Does that mean you'll come home?"

Hudson's smile fell. A sudden burst of suffocation hit, making him realize how trapped he had felt while living with Cage. "No. I can't go back to that. I can't risk that you'll go back inside your room and lock me out again. My chest feels like it's going to cave just thinking about it. I love you, but I need things to be different. You have all the power and I just have whatever you decide to give or take away. I don't want that anymore." He wouldn't accept that any longer. Cage would either love him back or he wouldn't. Hudson couldn't make anyone love him like they should. He had never had that power. But he was taking it back today. If Cage wanted them—he would fight. Otherwise, they really were done.

---

DESPERATION SCRATCHED AT CAGE'S INSIDES. He had done this. Ruined them. The rage Hudson had shown while yelling and beating his drone to death was beyond anything he had expected. Hudson was tiny, and—apparently—full of fury and fire. Cage truly hoped to find a way to turn that passion back his way. He tried staying calm. It wasn't Hudson's fault that Cage's life had ended years ago.

"Okay. I understand. For the record, I never meant to keep you prisoner. I thought you were happy with me. This darkness is the only life I have, and I can't choose to leave it, but you're right. You have a choice. I shouldn't have kept you trapped with me." Cage held tight to his cane and shifted positions. He would leave Hudson to be young and free. That was the right thing to do.

Hudson gently pushed Cage's cane aside before Cage could stand. The couch shifted beside him and then Hudson was there, straddling his lap. He was way too light. Someone so small shouldn't be so powerful, but he was. Hudson held Cage's heart in his palm. Cage was starting to feel like he should beg Hudson not to crush it.

Hudson's arms encircled his neck. His fingers found the ends of Cage's hair. He stroked. Cage almost purred. "Just because I didn't agree to come home doesn't mean I'm done with you."

"Oh." Cage didn't know where to put his hands.

"I want to kiss you."

"Okay. Well, I belong to you, so..." He was still trying to figure out what to do with his hands.

Hudson's breath fanned across his face. Cage

froze, silently begging. Hudson's lips touched his. Cage's arms closed around him, hauling him closer. Hudson's mouth opened over his. Cage took advantage and touched his tongue to Hudson's. Hudson shifted even closer. It was like feeling the sunshine after thirteen years of night.

"You're hard for me," Hudson said between kisses.

"I'm always hard for you."

An adorable-sounding chuckle vibrated against his lips. Hudson's hands slid down Cage's chest. "I've been right down the hall." His fingers moved lower. "All you had to do was come to me."

Cage grabbed Hudson's hands, stopping him from sneaking beneath Cage's shirt. "You don't want that, baby. There's nothing pretty underneath these clothes."

"How do you know how you look?" Hudson asked, sounding damnably levelheaded after their kiss.

"I endure the everyday pain and I can still feel. You don't want this."

Hudson crowded him, going chest to chest. His lips skimmed Cage's. "I want *you*. You're a not a *this*. You're a person. The man I love, to be specific. I wish you wouldn't try to decide for me."

"You promised." Cage hated to pull that low card, but Hudson had sworn he would let Cage keep his pride. Maybe it had been years since Hudson made that vow, but it still stood. Cage couldn't show this body to anyone. He couldn't.

"I don't want your pride, angel. Why don't you trust me?" The pain in Hudson's voice stole Cage's breath. "Just once, believe in me."

Cage could hear the despair and anger rising in Hudson's voice again. "There's no one else I trust more."

He felt the tension drain from Hudson. "I just want to hold you and maybe steal more kisses." Hudson's voice cracked, stealing Cage's heart. "You have no idea how much I've needed this."

Hudson didn't need to say more. Cage would hold him forever if Hudson wouldn't take his love away. He stroked Hudson's back and hair before sliding his fingers along Hudson's jaw. Damn. He was every bit as beautiful as Lynx described. The shape of his features had Cage mesmerized. He couldn't stop touching him and mapping his body. Hudson was hard for him too. That fascinated Cage. Only real love would make Hudson still want Cage after seeing him. "I love you. I'm sorry I made you feel like that's a lie. You're everything to me."

Hudson kissed the tips of Cage's fingers. He moved Cage's hand to his cheek and rubbed his cheek against Cage's palm like a dog. "I'm sorry I made you think I would ever choose anyone over you."

"We both know that was all my insecurities talking. You're no cheat." Cage had to be honest. Hudson deserved that.

Hudson's lips curved into a smile against his hand. "I guess we don't know how to disagree properly since we never have before. It's only natural for us to be bad at one thing."

Cage urged Hudson's mouth back to his. Now that he had Hudson in his arms, he didn't want to stop stealing all the affection he could get. Cage was starved for this. "We'll be perfect at everything else to make up for it." Hudson's kiss made Cage burn. He was so in love with Hudson that every touch was amazing. His body knew it was Hudson straddling him and wouldn't stop humming with delight. He stroked and massaged. Hudson moved restlessly against him. It was a proper make-out session. The inside of his underwear was a swamp of pre-cum. Their breaths sounded labored. He couldn't deny Hudson felt the same.

When Hudson settled against his chest and

buried his face against Cage's neck, Cage broke at the sensation of each breath caressing his throat. "Are you really going to make me go back home without you? I don't know if I can do it."

Hudson's lips lightly brushed his neck. "You're not going anywhere yet. I want to be held."

Cage squeezed Hudson a little tighter and settled in. Despite being turned on past the point of painful, Cage's heart won. He was content to be just like this. Long ago, he had accepted that he would never have this in his life again. He had gotten used to no one touching him—inasmuch as anyone could adjust to that. Now that he had Hudson, Cage couldn't stop the neediness from building and spilling out.

Hudson yawned so hard, his body shook a little with it.

A chuckle rumbled in Cage's throat. "I wore you out already, huh?"

"Sorry," Hudson mumbled, sounding half asleep already. "I don't think I've really slept at all since I moved here." He somehow managed to snuggle even closer to Cage. "This cuddling stuff is awesome."

Cage couldn't stop smiling. He gently stroked Hudson's back while soaking up the affection. Cage couldn't stay all night. He had meds he couldn't miss.

Cage wasn't free to do what he wanted: sit down and refuse to budge until Hudson came home. Surviving his injuries meant a life forever altered. He had oxygen treatments, skin treatments, and a handful of drugs to take. Cage would stay until he couldn't any longer, because his heart was under this roof. Tomorrow, he would start a new plan to be with Hudson. There had to be a way that wouldn't leave Hudson feeling trapped. Cage would find a way.

# EIGHT

AS THE SOUND of the doorbell rent the air, Cage froze. Without Hudson, Cage was trapped in darkness with no way to handle this situation. It couldn't be anyone he knew, because the door would've answered itself as they passed the facial recognition sensor. That meant there was a stranger at his door.

"Um," Cage said aloud, trying to decide what to do. "Charlie, open the intercom line for the front door."

"Front door intercom open."

"There's a drop box in the back for deliveries. Otherwise, no soliciting."

"I'm not here for that. This is Clint. Hudson's friend. I was hoping we could talk."

Damn. Cage tapped his foot. He hadn't expected this. If he turned Clint away and Clint told Hudson, this could set them back. That was the last thing Cage needed. He bit back an aggravated growl. Cage still didn't even know Hudson's new cellphone number. He couldn't risk anything else going wrong while he was still on such thin ice. "Charlie, open the front door. Clint, head to your right, and you'll see the kitchen. We can talk there."

"Thank you." Clint sounded genuinely relieved.

Cage waited. More than enough time passed for Clint to find the kitchen, but there was nothing but silence. "Are you there?"

"Oh," Clint said, sounding confused. "I was waiting for you to appear."

"I never see anyone in person."

Another stretch of silence met his confession. Cage almost asked if Clint left, when Clint finally spoke. "You never see anyone at all? Are you fucking kidding me? Is this really how you made Hudson live every day?"

A spark of anger lit in Cage's chest. This guy didn't know Cage. He didn't know what life was like for Cage. "Yet I still made him fall in love with me. Imagine that?"

"Huh," Clint said, sounding thoughtful. "Well, I

prefer a more man-to-man talk. If you really love Hudson and want him back, you should hear me out."

"I can hear you just fine from here."

"I guess Hudson is right to fear you'll never change. You can't even face me in the safety of your own home," Clint shot back just as quickly.

A growl escaped Cage. "Goddamn it. Give me a minute." Cage muttered to himself as he fought to pull on his thin gloves and hoodie, covering as much of his body as possible before finding his sunglasses. He couldn't believe he let Clint goad him into this, but fuck Clint. Cage loved Hudson and if Hudson wanted Cage to fight, he would.

After locating his cane, he made his way downstairs. At the kitchen door, he didn't stop to shake anyone's hand or even inquire if Clint was still there. He kept moving, heading for the living room. "We'll move to the couch where it's more comfortable."

"All right."

Cage fought a hint of panic at the response. Clint sounded big and too close. Cage was vulnerable here alone. He refused to show any weakness. He found the couch and sat. "I'm here. Say what you came to say."

"Okay." He felt the couch shift beside him as Clint sat. "You're right about me," he said fast—like ripping off a bandage. "When I first met Hudson, I wanted to be more than friends."

"You'd be crazy not to," Cage said, hoping to stay civil and meet Clint halfway.

Clint ignored his interruption. "At first, I didn't think of you as competition—only as his employer. But then we had dinner together and I saw something in him that I've only ever seen in one other person—damage that's caused by loving someone who will never love them back."

Cage's eyebrows rose as his temper threatened to snap. "I've done nothing but show my love for Hudson the past three years."

"Have you, though?" Before Cage could lose his shit completely, Clint pressed on. "Because the neglect is in his eyes. I would know; I broke the man I love in the same way." That took the wind from Cage's fury. Clint didn't stop there. "I watched the man I love struggle with my inability to give him the one thing he needed most—me. I took and took until he was all used up inside. Until he looked at someone else with all the love I never earned, because that person gave him what I couldn't— everything." Cage knew this story was true. The pain was in Clint's voice. "Now," Clint said, sounding determined. "I could do the same with Hudson. I could see his neglect and give him the affection you withheld, but I won't. I'm trying to be a good person. So I'm here instead. When my ex left me and married someone else, I sold everything and changed, even though it was too late for me to be the man he wanted. I hope I can be the man he wanted for the next guy who takes a chance on me, but I also get maybe no one else will ever take that chance again. Maybe everyone can take one look at me and see that I'm broken in some way that matters. I don't know, but you still have a shot. So you have to stop everything you've been doing and be different. Learn from my mistakes."

Cage wanted to say Clint's life wasn't his. He had given Hudson absolutely all he had to give, but his lips wouldn't shape that lie. Cage had listened while Hudson begged for him to hold him. He had heard the loneliness in Hudson's voice each time he recanted the events Cage made him attend. Each time, Cage had done nothing, because he had been scared to end up alone. He had been terrified Hudson would take one look at him and run away. In the end, Cage had ended up alone anyhow, and Hudson still hadn't rejected him when he showed himself. Cage knew he didn't deserve Hudson. The problem was, he equally didn't know how to win him back. He heard himself admitting as much to Clint.

"I've already been to see him and asked him to come home. He said no."

An ugly-sounding snort escaped Clint. "Did you really expect you could just show up one time and he would follow you home like a dog? It took you three years to drive him away. Hell, technically, you had to throw him out to get rid of him. You'll have to work harder to undo that much damage."

In his aggravation, Cage revealed too much. "I have literally nothing to fight with. All I have is money, and Hudson isn't moved by that."

He heard Clint take a deep breath. It was obvious he wasn't used to talking about feelings. "If the man I love had left me and I knew where to find him and I thought I had a chance in hell with him, I know what I'd do. He'd trip over me everywhere he went. I would be right there all the time. He would see my face and I would tell him all the things I didn't know how to say. I destroyed any shot of doing those things. You haven't. You're not dead, Cage. Stop living like you are. Hudson loves you. I can see it in his eyes every time he says your name. Even though you tried to kill his feelings, he isn't done yet."

Cage had no intention of stopping. He just didn't know if he was brave enough to do the one thing he had left to do in this fight. Cage had lived in this house for a decade. It was his security blanket, wired to serve his needs. But if Hudson needed life to be different, Cage would give up everything for him. It was time to go all in or lose him.

---

EVERY DAY SINCE CAGE HAD GIVEN UP ON LIFE, Lynx had shown up and tried to convince him to keep trying. Cage was Lynx's best friend. His chosen family. Keeping Cage alive since his life ended had been a constant challenge. He had found a way to give him a purpose with their gaming company and they had worked together to make his house so smart that Cage didn't need his vision. But convincing him to hire Hudson had been his greatest accomplishment with Cage. Hudson had been the exact miracle Cage and Lynx needed. Hudson falling in love with Cage, in spite of Cage's every barrier between them, that was just a goddamn miracle. Lynx couldn't let Cage throw that away. So

Lynx planned to keep showing up every damn day until Hudson came home. He knew in his heart, as long as Cage kept trying, Hudson would eventually come home.

Cage and Lynx had been friends since they were five. They had met their first day at an elite private school. Neither of them fit in. Even though Lynx's father owned one of the largest tech companies in the world and Cage's father was a renowned scientist who worked for the government, they didn't match with the other over-privileged kids. They hadn't been spoiled or raised by nannies. But they had something else too. Something that made them just a little different. Neither of them had realized it until they kissed at twelve.

Before Cage's attack, he had easily been one of the most beautiful boys Lynx had ever seen. Blond hair, perfect angles, and the lightest eyes. To his soul, Lynx believed that was one of the reasons he had been attacked. He had made at least one of those boys have feelings he didn't want. God knew, Cage had made Lynx have feelings he didn't want, but that was a different story.

Now, nearly thirteen years after Cage's whole life changed, he was still beautiful to Lynx. Ending up scarred hadn't changed the thing that made Cage so stunning—his heart. That heart was set on Hudson. So, Hudson it would get, if Lynx had to drag him back home.

As Lynx steered his twenty-year-old Honda Civic into Cage's driveway, he parked next to an unfamiliar truck. Even though it looked brand new, the tires were muddy—like it came from a farm. Lynx's curiosity had him moving faster than usual and Lynx was always moving at top speed. He had shit to do.

After circling the house, he took the front steps two at a time. Since Lynx had helped build Cage's security system, the door automatically opened as he came into view of the camera. It was programmed to allow exactly three people inside. Lynx had to bring that third home. Voices reached him before he reached the living room. A deep southern drawl caressed Lynx's ears before he cleared the doorway. Amber eyes turned his way as he stepped inside. The man stood. Lynx swallowed. He had to tilt his chin up to keep holding the guy's stare. He was huge, red-haired, and looking at Lynx in a way that stole Lynx's thoughts.

"Hey," the guy said, sounding uncomfortable. He held a cowboy hat between his hands.

"Hi." Lynx felt like an idiot. He was never at a

loss for words. Cage had actually been sitting and visiting with this guy. Cage never accepted visitors.

Cage motioned the guy's way. "Lynx, this is Clint. Clint, this is my best friend and business partner, Lynx Hirata."

The gigantic cowboy held his hand out. "Nice to meet you."

This was Clint? The Clint? The man who had come between Hudson and Cage? Goddamn. Cage was right to worry. His hand was engulfed as he accepted Clint's handshake. "You, as well." For a moment, neither of them released the other. Their gazes held. Lynx swore something passed between them—like a shot of electricity ran up Lynx's arm. He was slightly mesmerized. He cleared his throat and forced his eyes and hand from Clint. Lynx focused on Cage. "I just came by to grab Hudson's keys so I can take him his car like we discussed."

At just the sound of Hudson's name, a small smile immediately appeared on Cage's lips. "I'm not sure where they are. Charlie, track Hudson's keys."

"Hudson's keys are in the kitchen."

Clint's eyebrows rose and he glanced around, looking impressed. Lynx couldn't stop himself from bragging. "Charlie is a smart-home system Cage and I designed. He's similar to what's already on the market but way more sophisticated. Of course, he's also a bit too expensive for most people. There's no way to make him economical enough for mass market production." Clint was all hard angles and keen eyes. He made Lynx a tad uncomfortable. It wasn't entirely in a bad way. Lynx cleared his throat again. "I'll just grab those keys." Lynx made quick work of finding Hudson's keys. He didn't want Clint to slip away before he could get a look at the backside of him. Lynx's footsteps slowed as he slipped back inside the living room. Clint faced Cage with his back to the kitchen, and goddamn. His ass was every bit as squeezable as Lynx suspected. Clint glanced over his shoulder. Lynx had a bad feeling he was busted. He fought the heat creeping up his face.

Lynx chose to pretend nothing happened. "I was thinking, I should grab Hudson some flowers from you on the way. That way, when he brings me back to my car... if he brings me back to my car, he'll have a reason to come in and thank you."

Clint nodded. "Yes. You should do that but let me give you my number in case Hudson refuses to give you a lift back. I'll come pick you up."

Lynx bit his bottom lip, trying not to smile like an idiot. "Good idea."

Since Cage was blind, he was oblivious to the

heated glances. His forehead furrowed. "I don't know that Hudson would fall for flowers. That's a bit cliché, don't you think?"

Clint seemed to be trying to get them back together too. He didn't back down. "Cliché is exactly why you should do it. Those small things are always done because they haven't stopped being nice gestures. Even if he doesn't get excited over the flowers, I'm willing to bet it's still points in your favor."

Cage spent a moment chewing on his lip. Finally, he gave a sharp nod. "Take him some roses from the yard instead. He loves those rose bushes and those are more personal than me just throwing more money at him. He'll probably already be pissed about the car. I'm really at a point where I can't do anything right in his eyes."

Clint pulled a pained face but didn't say a word. That was enough to let Lynx know Cage had fucked up more than they could even imagine by putting Hudson out. He had broken something. It was obvious Clint wasn't sure it could be fixed. But Clint was here, and Lynx would take that as hope. He couldn't let his best friend give up. If Cage lost hope of winning back Hudson, he might quit life altogether and Lynx couldn't live with that outcome.

"If you're headed out now, I'll cut those roses for you."

Clint's offer had Lynx feeling selfish. While there was still work to do with Hudson and Cage, he wanted to spend a few more minutes basking in Clint's sexiness. A flirtatious smile pulled at Lynx's lips. It was out of his control. "I would appreciate that. Plus, I still need to grab your number."

Clint's mouth lifted in one corner. His eyes didn't soften. Lynx's breath left his lungs in a whoosh. Clint was hard on the inside. Lynx could feel the darkness pulsing from him. He was the kind of man who held someone's throat while fucking them hard from behind. Lynx loved that. He swore, the minute Cage was back in good hands, Lynx would concentrate on himself. If and when that day came, Clint just might be in a bit of trouble. He was in Lynx's sights now.

---

THE PRIME LOCATION OF HUDSON'S RENTAL WAS perfect for walking to the store. Until he started a new job, he wouldn't need a car. He was used to not going anywhere. Living with Cage had taken him from being an introvert to a hermit. For the most part, he was used to being alone. The silence was murder, though. Hudson missed the sound of Cage's voice filling every room. He wasn't loving that. His lips automatically curved into a smile at just the thought of Cage. He had woken up on the couch alone, but a new broom with a red ribbon tied around it had sat nearby waiting. Hudson didn't know how Cage did any of things he did, but he never ceased to amaze Hudson.

As Hudson turned the corner to his house, he spotted Lynx on his porch first. That was odd, considering Hudson's car was in the driveway. He should have spotted that first. A huge smile spread across Lynx's face—like he was happy to see Hudson. Hudson shifted his bag from one arm to the other in a show of nerves.

Lynx didn't seem put off by Hudson's lack of greeting. "Hey, gorgeous. I delivered your car."

"You can take it back."

Lynx's smile grew. "Nope. Your name is on the title. No take backs. I do need a lift to Cage's, though. That's where I left my car."

Hudson pressed his lips together. He didn't know whether to laugh or rage. Instead, he blew out a sigh. "Yeah, okay. Just let me put these groceries in the kitchen and we'll go."

Lynx jumped to his feet. The light caught his diamond nose ring, making it glimmer. As he followed Hudson inside, Hudson tried to ignore his overwhelming presence, but Lynx wasn't having it. His usual overabundance of energy filled the kitchen. "So," Lynx said, dragging out the word. "What's Clint like?"

Hudson's eye twitched. "For fuck's sake. We're only friends."

"I know."

Lynx's automatic answer—like he didn't even need to think about it—had Hudson's ire falling away. Still, he checked Lynx's expression for any hint of disapproval before saying anything. "Thank you for that. He's a nice person. A little stern, and I think a lot lonely, but nice."

Lynx nodded while looking thoughtful. "Cage can't see himself and he lives in constant pain," Lynx said fast—like determined to have his say. "All he has to go by is the way he feels, so he thinks he looks as terrible as he feels. That makes him a lot more insecure than he should be."

Hudson concentrated on putting up his groceries. That made sense and wasn't surprising. Still, Hudson wanted more of Lynx's insight. No one knew Cage like Lynx. "What was he like before the attack?"

"Beautiful."

Hudson shot him an annoyed look. "He's still beautiful."

A bright smile lit Lynx's face. "I know. I meant that he was the type of person who invoked jealousy without him having to do a thing. He was sexy, came from a rich family, and he was smarter than everyone else. Above all else, he was kind. I know he's still all those things, but he didn't even know he was those things back then. That made him twice as hard to resist. Now he's just a mess."

Hudson thought that over while he put away the last of his groceries. He could see Cage being everything Lynx described. Neither of them spoke again until they were headed for the front door.

Lynx passed Hudson his keys. "You'll need these."

Heartache choked Hudson as his fingers closed around the key to the car Cage had bought him. "If I keep this car, he'll always wonder if I only stuck around for the gifts he gave."

Lynx stopped. He looked sad. "You say that as if you never plan to take him back."

Hudson kept his gaze averted and headed for the

car. "I can't go back to living the way we did." He opened the driver's side door. Three pink roses from Cage's rose bushes were on the seat. Hudson's eyes stung as he moved them to the console. Cage knew him too well. He knew how much Hudson loved that house and those goddamn bushes.

"You've seen him now. He won't go back to shutting you out." Hudson wasn't so sure. It was easy to fall back into old habits. Lynx waited to strike again until Hudson was driving too fast to shove him out without landing a murder charge. "Of course, you could have pushed your way into his room any time in the last three years and left Cage no choice but to accept your love, but you didn't. So I don't think he's the only one who's been hiding."

To Hudson's surprise, the accusation didn't bother him. If Lynx had ever bothered to ask Hudson why he didn't force his way in, he would've answered a long time ago. "Cage has only ever asked for one promise from me—to let him keep his pride. I freely admit I've begged him to see me, but I never stole that one thing from him. If he hadn't come to see me freely, I never would have."

"Damn," Lynx said, sounding blown away. "You really do love him."

Hudson flashed Lynx an annoyed look. "Duh."

"I'm sorry that I had days when I doubted you."

Hudson nodded. That was fair. Lynx was Cage's best friend. It was his job to protect Cage. "I'm sorry he never loved you back the way you've loved him."

A chuckle escaped Lynx. "Cage was blind long before he was blind, but truthfully, I've always needed his friendship more. He's the only person I haven't thoroughly disappointed. If he had given me his heart, I would have let him down too."

"Maybe you should change your shirt," Hudson offered, hoping to lighten the mood. Lynx dressed like a homeless person and drove a twenty-year-old car. Hudson had never understood why a man who owned a multi-million-dollar company lived like he was dirt poor.

"I like this shirt." The muttered words sounded childish, making Hudson smile.

"So do moths, apparently."

A loud and heavy sigh rang out, filling the car. "You don't understand nerdom at all," Lynx said, taking the bait and becoming the ridiculous guy he always was. "You don't throw away your favorite TV show's shirt because it has a few stains or holes. It's *vintage*. Honestly, I don't know what Cage sees in you. Is there a single thing that causes you to geek out or do you just sort of exist in a perfect bubble? If I hadn't played games with you, I would think you had never seen a gaming system. You have no culture. Seriously, just one comic con. That's all I'm asking. Go to just one dressed as your favorite character and you'll be a furry for life."

"Wait. What?" Hudson put the car in park in Cage's driveway. "Are you a furry?"

"Everyone's a furry. How could you not be an enthusiast for animals with human-like qualities. Haven't you ever eaten at the pizza place with the rat? That place is fucking awesome."

"That's not what a furry is."

Lynx's exasperation was hilarious. Hudson couldn't stop smiling while Lynx gestured wildly with his hands. "Of course it is. Look it up. That's literally the definition of a furry."

Hudson shook his head and opened his door, grabbing his flowers as he slid from the car. "I'm absolutely not looking that up and getting put on some government pervert list." He stopped when he realized Lynx wasn't following him to the door. "Are you not going to say hi to Cage while you're here?"

"Nah," Lynx said, flashing him a smile. He motioned toward his car. "I have a business meeting in a bit. Plus, I saw him earlier, but you should still go. You need to put those flowers in some water and thank Cage for them properly and all that."

Hudson shrugged. Lynx had always been weird. After all, he had been born Joseph and changed his name to Lynx—of all things—the minute he turned eighteen. If that didn't describe exactly how strange Lynx was, Hudson didn't know what did. "All right. I'll see you later, I guess."

Lynx gave him an awkward head bob. "Yep. Be thinking about that costume. You're going to the next convention."

With an eye roll, Hudson turned away and headed for the house. His bad nerves didn't set in until Hudson stepped onto the porch. He didn't know if he should knock or what. The door had always automatically opened for him. Hudson imagined Cage disabled that when he fired Hudson. To his surprise, the door swung wide—the way it always did. Still, Hudson tapped his knuckles on the door as he stepped inside.

"It's me. I didn't want to drop Lynx off and not say hi." Hudson fully expected to hear Cage's voice spilling from the speakers, as usual.

Instead, Cage stepped from the kitchen. "Hey, beautiful."

Hudson's heart had his eyes eating alive the sight

of Cage. He still had thin gloves covering his hands and he wore a long-sleeved turtleneck. Plus, sunglasses covered his eyes just as they had last time, but the hoodie was gone. Cage had thick and shiny blond hair that was swept to one side. It looked long enough to put in a short ponytail. Hudson wanted to touch it.

He had to take a breath before he could speak. "Hey, gorgeous. I got your roses."

A small smile hovered on his lips. "I thought you could keep them at your place. In case you're missing your rose bushes."

Hudson fought the urge to shift nervously. He felt out of place in the house that had once been a home. "Okay... well." He shifted toward the door. He didn't want to leave, but neither did he feel like he should stay.

"Would you be upset if I sold this house?"

For a full minute, Hudson's brain froze, refusing to free his tongue. When he finally found his voice, his words came out sounding outraged. "Why would you do that? This place is wired for you. You'd have to adjust to whole new surroundings. That's a lot of work when you have such a great house already."

Cage's chin was tilted slightly toward the floor— like he thought carefully about every word Hudson said before answering. "You've put my comfort first for the past three years. It's time for you to come first. As long as I'm living here, I don't think you'll come home. Maybe this place is only a prison to you. If that's the case, I'd rather have to adjust to a new place than have to adjust to a life without you."

Hudson closed the door. He couldn't leave now. "Can I see your room?"

Cage had the sweetest smile. It melted Hudson's heart as it appeared. "If you'd like. Lead the way."

Without a word, Hudson set his roses on the coffee table and headed for the stairs. He could feel Cage at his back as he climbed each step. Cage's bedroom door stood open. Hudson hesitated inside the doorway. The room was huge. It took up almost the entire second floor. One side was Cage's workspace. Hudson headed there first. He ran his hand over the blank keys of Cage's keyboard. A smile curved his lips as he felt the tiny bumps. Cage was scary smart. He imagined it had taken him no time at all to learn Braille. Every computer component imaginable sat in Cage's space. Everything was set up to accommodate him and his limitations, becoming an extension of him.

Hudson moved to the treadmill next. It too was made to be easily controlled by touch alone. There was a refrigerator and microwave between the workspace and bed. Beyond the bed was a bathroom that looked similar to Hudson's. Large with a walk-in shower, except there were also guide rails. Hudson sat on the foot of the king-sized bed. He immediately sank into the plush mattress. The dark blue comforter was in a heap to one side of the bed. The same speaker system that sat next to Hudson's bed also sat next to Cage's. Cage stood quietly, holding his cane and waiting for Hudson to finish exploring. Hudson stared at him. There was so much love inside Hudson's chest for this man who was still more of a mystery than Hudson cared to admit.

"It's so strange to me that I did countless things, thinking you were watching." Hudson's gaze swung toward the workstation. There were security monitors showing different parts of the house and driveway, but nothing like what Hudson had always pictured. "I don't know how to feel, I guess."

"Did you like the idea of me watching you?"

Hudson didn't need to think about it. "I liked the idea that I was pleasing you. My whole life, no one wanted me. Then I came here, and you did." Hudson shrugged, feeling exposed. "I liked that I seemed to make you happy."

Cage nodded. "But were you happy? Or were you just grateful to have a home?"

Hudson gave Cage's question the thought it deserved. "It was the happiest I ever felt, but there was always something missing. How much do you want for the house?"

Cage looked taken aback by the sudden topic change. "I don't know. I assume I'll have to have it appraised and all that."

"I'll pay you fifty thousand for you to stay in it," Hudson said with no real plan. "I'd offer to buy the place, but I still have to survive until I find a job, and I doubt anyone would finance me to buy this place."

"I don't want your money."

Hudson's hands lifted before falling back to his lap, because—honestly—he had nothing. "I mean, really, it's your money anyhow. I didn't earn it."

Cage crossed the room and sat on the bed beside Hudson. "You did, but let's compromise. I'll stay if you move back. You keep *your* money and I'll share my bedroom with you."

Hudson pretended to think it over. "What if you share your bedroom with me, and I use the money to get us a pool? I'd planned to talk to you about that before everything fell apart."

It was almost funny the way Cage appeared to

truly consider his counteroffer. Hudson couldn't stop smiling as he stared at Cage's profile. "How about I share my room and pay for the pool? You keep your money and marry me? That way, it's our money, our house, and you can make whatever additions you want."

Hudson settled onto his back and stared at the ceiling. He toyed with the belt loop on the back of Cage's jeans while he pretended to think about it. "What if we do all those things and you let me take you to dinner tonight?" Because Hudson had to know now if he would be trapped doing everything alone for the rest of his life while Cage hid.

"How about we do all that, I pay for dinner, and you let me make love to you?"

Hudson's heart skipped a beat. His mouth went dry. He refused to show any nerves. "Will you ever let me pay for anything?"

"No. Will you ever answer my question?"

Despite his best efforts, when Hudson took a deep breath, it sounded shaky, giving him away. "As much as I've done, thinking you were watching, you know I've never actually been with anyone. Sexually, that is. Not that I don't want to," he quickly added before Cage had time to think he was being rejected.

"Do you trust me?"

Hudson didn't hesitate. "Yes."

"Then what's your answer?"

Hudson pressed his hand to his stomach. He counted to seven in his head, giving himself exactly seven seconds to freak out, before speaking. "I'll move back, marry you, let you buy the pool, pay for dinner, and make love to me. Wait," he said, blinking as it dawned on him that he had—somehow—let Cage have everything. "I thought we were compromising."

Cage turned and crawled onto the bed. He moved, feeling his way around until he straddled Hudson's body. "We did. We're both getting everything we want. I won't let you down. You'll see."

Hudson believed. There was no one he trusted more. If Cage said he wouldn't fail Hudson, then he wouldn't. Plus, it was really hard to doubt Cage while staring up at him. Hudson was too busy trying not to think with his dick.

---

Hudson felt great beneath him. Cage couldn't wait to have him nude. In truth, he was a bit nervous. It wasn't like he was the most experienced guy on the planet. But Cage had years of built-up fantasies and he had a feeling this was the best way to convince Hudson he wouldn't go back to locking himself away. Plus, he really wanted Hudson.

He slowly lowered his head. Hudson met him halfway. Their lips met. For a second, their kiss was so sweet that Cage's eyes burned. Then, passion exploded. Cage bit at Hudson's lips and kissed him deeply. His body automatically moved against Hudson's, seeking relief from years of pent-up longing. Cage tore at Hudson's clothes and kissed every place he could reach until not a stitch of Hudson's clothing remained.

"I need your help," Cage said, sounding winded and turned on even to his ears.

Hudson didn't let him down. "Of course."

Cage desperately wanted the kinky Hudson. The one who hadn't minded performing on camera, thinking Cage watched. "Find the lube on my bedside table and get ready for me. I need you to do the things I can't see to do."

A sexy rumble of laughter caressed his ears. "Am I back to giving you a show?"

A hum escaped Cage without his permission. There was the Hudson he needed. "Just a small one." He rolled to one side, setting Hudson free.

"Don't be afraid to use your words so I can picture everything you're doing."

He felt the bed shift as Hudson did as Cage asked. "You look so turned on right now. How slick do you want this hole?"

The air was so thick with desire that Cage could barely breathe. "Really slick. I want to make you scream but not in pain." He unbuttoned and unzipped his pants, setting his erection free.

"Goddamn, Cage. You're incredibly sexy. I can't believe you spent the last three years hiding from me. I'm not complaining, because I don't regret a thing about falling in love with you, but wow. You have no idea how much you're wanted."

Cage couldn't call Hudson a liar. There was too much desire in his voice to deny. But love was blind, and Cage didn't believe for a second Hudson would have fallen for him if he had seen him first. Cage stroked his cock. "Come straddle my hips, beautiful," Cage said, hoping Hudson was ready. Hudson immediately obeyed. Cage played with Hudson's dick, massaging and teasing until Hudson moved against his hand and his breathing turned ragged. "I want you to be in control. Don't worry about pleasing me. Just take what you want, understood?"

Hudson didn't respond right away. He rubbed

Cage's torso while sitting quietly on Cage's hips. "But I want to please you," he said finally.

"Then do as I say and use me. Don't think. Just feel. I can't see you. You can do whatever you want without an audience." Cage swore he felt the air change—like something he said made Hudson even hotter.

Hudson shifted positions and palmed Cage's cock. He almost came the minute Hudson's small hand squeezed him. He needed Hudson to take what he wanted. Cage was too desperate for him. If Cage took charge, he might hurt Hudson in his madness. He needed Hudson to find what felt good to him. Hudson rubbed Cage's crown against his asshole. Cage tried breathing slowly through his nose. His entire body seized as Hudson pressed down, taking him inside just a hair. Hudson gasped at the intrusion. Cage stroked Hudson's cock, trying to distract him. A moan escaped Hudson and Cage quickened his pace. This would be a short encounter for Cage. Hudson needed to come quickly. Hudson rocked, taking Cage a little deeper. Cage ground his back teeth. Hudson was so hot and tight. He was tiny and Cage was ready to blow. Cage pumped at Hudson's erection. He felt Hudson's body tense. A gasp reverberated off the walls and Hudson pressed down, impaling himself.

Cage's lungs stopped working. Hudson's body tried sucking him deeper as Hudson came, soaking Cage's shirt with cum. The pressure he had been fighting exploded. Cage dug his heels into the mattress and tried getting even deeper inside Hudson. Cries tore from his throat. Hudson fell forward and captured Cage's lips, swallowing the noises he made. Logically, Cage recognized that this was Hudson's first time and Cage's first time in many years, and likely wasn't that great for Hudson, but Cage felt something change between them. It was like they grew or broke through some invisible barrier, becoming more together. Their kiss turned sweet. Their tongues brushed like it was a silent promise. They were in this life together. Their bodies, hearts, and souls were connected. Cage had been stupid to not trust Hudson's love for him. It had nothing to do with Hudson. Cage had been weak and given Hudson less than he deserved. It wouldn't happen again.

"I love you," Cage whispered against Hudson's lips, needing him to feel it.

Hudson didn't hesitate to give the words back. "I love you too."

Since Cage was a mess to his core, some insecurities immediately tried creeping back in the second he came down from the rush. "It'll get better. I just need you to adjust because I can't stand the idea of hurting you."

Hudson chuckled. The sound vibrated against Cage's lips as Hudson tried to steal more kisses. "You think too much. I'm in heaven right now, so hush and let me enjoy it."

Cage forced his brain to be quiet. They had their whole lives. He believed in Hudson's love, even if Cage couldn't trust his own confidence to hold. Hudson wouldn't leave him. This was real. They were real. Hudson had agreed to marry him. Happiness poured through Cage. He rolled, pinning Hudson beneath him and deepening their kiss. This man had truly agreed to be his husband. The reality of that was huge. He couldn't wait for the whole world to know this one belonged to him. Cage hadn't earned him, but he would. Hudson would be the happiest husband on earth, because Cage wouldn't have it any other way.

# NINE

CONSIDERING how out of place Hudson had felt while staying at his temporary lodgings, Hudson expected to be disoriented when he woke in Cage's bed. Instead, not only had he slept later than he had in ages, Hudson felt like he was home. Cage had still been sleeping when Hudson woke. He was so peaceful looking that Hudson slipped from the bed and headed downstairs without waking him. In a happy dream-like haze, Hudson moved around the kitchen making breakfast. This was the life he had wanted for them. For the first time, it felt real.

"Cage is up for the day."

At Charlie's set announcement that had kept him on task when he had been Cage's caretaker, Hudson nearly stamped his foot. "Damn." He had wanted to surprise Cage with breakfast in bed. Instead, it looked like it would just have to be breakfast together. At that thought, Hudson almost danced in place. He felt all his dreams snapping into place. No one knew how long he had craved an ordinary life. Hudson hadn't felt the least bit normal in years.

With a simple breakfast complete, Hudson gathered everything onto a tray and sent it up the dumbwaiter so he wouldn't have to carry it up the stairs before meeting it up there. The bathroom door stood open and steam rolled out. A smile tugged at Hudson's lips. He tried to ignore the wave of relief washing over him. There had been a tiny sliver of fear that he would find the door barred against him again. That would have destroyed him.

After retrieving the food and coffee, Hudson set it on the bedside table before going after his man. He peeked inside the bathroom. Surprise held him in place. Cage stood at the sink with only a towel wrapped around his hips. Hudson realized he had been unprepared. Cage was missing part of an arm. Hudson hadn't even realized one of Cage's hands was fake. His scars made him look like his skin had been ripped away. There was a pattern to them—like Cage had been standing when the gasoline had been poured down his back. Tears filled Hudson's eyes. His throat swelled. He couldn't imagine the nightmare Cage had endured. The suffering he still endured. Hudson covered his mouth and silently backed away. He wouldn't let Cage know he had seen. One day, Hudson swore Cage wouldn't even think about his appearance any longer in Hudson's presence. He would live freely and unhidden. Until then, Hudson would love him like he deserved. He sat on the bed and waited. He would start giving Cage everything he had today. Cage was the love of his life. Hudson wouldn't let him ever doubt that again.

---

CAGE SCRUBBED AT HIS WET HAIR WITH A TOWEL as he headed back inside the bedroom. In all likelihood, his hair stood in every direction now. It was easy not to care since he couldn't see it. He had a shit ton of work to get through this morning if he hoped to spend the rest of the day trying to convince Hudson to bring his stuff back home. Cage wouldn't believe Hudson for real intended to move back until his things were back beneath Cage's roof. But damn, he had loved holding Hudson all night. There was a happy hum inside Cage today he couldn't shake. He hadn't thought it was possible to love Hudson more, but he did today.

"Goddamn. Look at all that sexiness."

Cage froze as Hudson's voice washed over him. His arms and hands weren't covered. He hated the idea of Hudson seeing him like this. Cage held completely still—as if he expected Hudson couldn't still see him if he didn't move—like Hudson was a t-rex or something.

"Come here."

Damn. The lust in Hudson's voice had Cage moving toward him without thought. At the edge of the bed, Hudson's hands slid across Cage's hips. His lips caressed Cage's stomach. Since it was too late to hide, Cage stole his chance to finally feel Hudson's hair with no gloves between them. Soft curls slipped through his fingers. They were so thick. Cage was captivated by Hudson's hair. Lynx's descriptions didn't do Hudson justice.

Hudson stroked Cage's ass. "I want to do something, but I've never done it before, so I probably won't be very good at it."

Cage's brain misfired. He hoped Hudson meant what Cage thought he meant. "I'm yours to do with as you please."

Hudson kissed Cage's stomach again. "Am I keeping you from anything besides the breakfast I made?"

Cage shook his head. He wasn't stupid enough to answer any other way.

Hudson's hands moved from Cage's ass to the front of his jeans. "I could let you eat first," he said as he unbuttoned and unzipped Cage's jeans.

"Are you teasing? I can't tell."

An evil-sounding chuckle caressed his ears. "Yes. The bulge staring me in the face says everything I need to know." Hudson set his erection free. Cage sucked in a sharp breath as Hudson lightly licked his crown. "You'll probably get tired of me being mediocre at everything, but you're impossible for me to resist." Hudson punctuated his claim by sucking the tip of Cage's cock. The air thinned. Cage swore the room spun.

"If this is mediocre, I won't survive a higher level of expertise."

Hudson didn't hold back. He licked and sucked, making Cage half insane with lust. Cage lost his patience a few minutes in and took Hudson down on the mattress. He tugged and pulled until he had Hudson nude. At one point, he kneed Hudson in the forehead as he impatiently went all in until he had

Hudson's cock in his mouth and Hudson was back to sucking him. Cage didn't doubt they would laugh about his crazed attempt to have his way with Hudson later, but Cage couldn't help himself. He hadn't realized how badly he wanted this life until Hudson gave it to him. This was happiness. He hadn't known it could be like this. Cage didn't think about how he looked. It never crossed his mind that Hudson might be turned off by him. Hudson's body told the real story. He couldn't fake the way his dick leaked in Cage's mouth.

It was easy to forget all the insecurities that held him back when Hudson touched him. Pressure climbed his shaft. Cage mindlessly sucked Hudson's cock as he reached for the orgasm Hudson's mouth promised. A half second before he exploded, Cage pulled away and covered his dick with his shirt, refusing to make Hudson choke on his cum. The bite of Hudson's fingernails in the back of Cage's thighs let him know Hudson wasn't thrilled with that decision, but even in the rush of his euphoric high, Cage didn't stop trying to suck the cum from Hudson. A cry escaped Hudson. Hot jets of semen filled Cage's mouth. He hummed as he swallowed. Hudson babbled his love and other things Cage couldn't understand as he scratched at Cage's skin.

He chuckled, feeling triumphant as he switched positions. Without thought, he whipped his shirt up and over his head and kicked out of his pants. He didn't want to soak Hudson's skin as he straddled the man's body. It wasn't until he lowered his mouth to Hudson's and their chests met that Cage realized what he had done. He snagged the comforter and covered them. Even though Cage couldn't completely hide, he would do what he could to save Hudson from the sight of him. Hudson didn't seem to notice one way or the other. He was too busy stroking Cage every place he could reach while struggling to catch his breath.

"Wow." Hudson kissed his chest and shoulder. "I'm blown away by you." He chuckled. "Your breakfast is probably ruined."

A smile popped to Cage's lips. "Totally worth it. I just had an even better meal."

"Oh, shit. Sorry, guys."

They froze for half a second as Lynx's voice cut through their bubble of happiness before Hudson scrambled to ensure they were completely covered. They had been so focused on each other, they hadn't heard the alarm disarm.

"I'll wait downstairs," Lynx said before either of them could respond to his sudden arrival. The sound of his booted feet rushing back down the stairs pulled a chuckle from Cage.

Hudson's entire body shook beneath him with silent laughter. "Oh my god. What if he had been like five minutes earlier?"

The sensation of Hudson hiding against Cage's chest—like he subconsciously sought Cage's protection—had Cage swelling with pride. There was no one else like the man beneath him. Cage would keep him safe—even if it was only from prying eyes. "Don't worry. I'll set some boundaries with Lynx. He's used to us being up a lot earlier than this."

Hudson's lips skimmed Cage's neck, making chill bumps rise on his skin. Butterflies stirred in Cage's stomach. "It's fine. As much as I want to keep you right here forever, I know you need to work."

An out-of-control smile hit from nowhere. Cage fought the urge to bounce on the bed like a little kid who had too much sugar. It was like reality smacked him in the face all over again. Hudson loved him. Cage wanted to tell the whole world. "Let's get dressed. I want to tell Lynx we're getting married. Hell, let's go get married right now."

Hudson's body shook harder beneath him. He swore he could feel the happiness in Hudson's laughter. "You know there's a waiting period in Texas, right?"

Cage wouldn't be denied. He was too excited. "There's no waiting period in Vegas, where I'm from. You can meet my parents and we could be married by the end of the day."

"Are you really going from never seeing anyone to getting on a plane filled with people?"

Hudson's question brought a bit of reality back to Cage, but he still wasn't deterred. "Say yes and I'll do whatever it takes."

"Yes."

Hudson tossed the covers aside. "Charlie, tell Lynx I'm getting married."

A half second passed before a loud and happy-sounding shout came from downstairs. Hudson chuckled. The sound filled Cage to overflowing. He was ready to have the best life ever. With Hudson, he felt freed from his cage. With Hudson, Cage believed anything was possible. He wanted to get started right away on living again. He wanted this life with Hudson.

# TEN

WHILE SITTING on Cage's knee, Hudson watched images move across his computer screen on one side while meaningless html ran on the other side. Each time Cage spoke a new line into his mic, the image moved and did something else, creating a character adventure before his eyes. It was fascinating watching Cage work. He had no clue how Cage did this, and then adding in that he couldn't see, the game creation became almost hypnotizing.

"This is like watching a magic show. Even though I'm watching it happen, I still have no idea how you're doing it."

"I played games a lot as a kid, so I can kind of see the images in my head as the computer reads my notes to me through the earbuds. The right keystrokes are just second nature to me. Of course, I'm also super dependent on you and other alpha players, playing the game and finding the glitches I can't see."

Hudson shook his head. "That's not really what I meant. You're too smart for me. I have no idea how all those letters and symbols become the games I play with Lynx. It's fascinating."

"Speaking of Lynx," Cage said, ignoring Hudson's praise the way he always did. "What's he doing now?"

Hudson stood and moved to the bedroom window. He stayed out of sight as he peeked out. A chuckle escaped him at the show below. White chairs, tables, and a flowered archway littered the backyard. None of that had a thing to do with his humor. In fact, the sight of his wedding coming together made Hudson want to do a happy dance. He hadn't thought he could love Cage more until it truly hit him they would be married soon.

For all of Cage's enthusiasm to get married right away, realistically, he hadn't been able to leave town due to his medical issues. Once they calmed down, the reality of that had set in. They had settled for applying for their marriage license and moving Hudson's things home. The three-day waiting period had been hell on Hudson's nerves, and he had no idea why. It was like his life felt like a dream now. He expected to wake any moment and find himself back in his short-term rental with no hope for his broken heart. Hudson couldn't stop following Cage around the house like a lovesick puppy. Thankfully, Cage hadn't tired of him yet.

"What's that chuckle about?"

Hudson forced his attention back to Lynx and Clint in the backyard at Cage's question. "Lynx looks like he's talking a mile a minute while trying and failing to climb a tree. Clint looks as harsh as ever while watching him—like the most put upon man you've ever seen."

Hudson glanced over his shoulder. Cage's smile caught and held Hudson's attention. He forgot Lynx's wild attempts to find any excuse to catch Clint's interest. "Poor Lynx. I don't think I've ever seen him this desperate for anyone's attention."

Hudson shook his head. It seemed Cage still had no idea that Lynx had tried for years to catch Cage's attention. But Hudson got what he meant; Lynx truly seemed to like Clint. Hudson was glad to see it. They both needed someone in their lives.

Cage stood and closed the distance between them. He crowded Hudson's space, pulling Hudson back against his chest. His lips brushed Hudson's nape. "Does it look like they'll be finished putting together the perfect backyard wedding for us anytime soon?" His hand slipped beneath Hudson's shirt, leaving no question as to why he asked. Hudson wasn't the only one of them who couldn't seem to get enough.

"We could just lock the door and steal some time alone," Hudson suggested, sneaking his hand between their bodies, cupping Cage's cock and massaging.

Cage nibbled his ear, making chill bumps rise on Hudson's skin. "I locked the door ten minutes ago to keep my parents out." He chuckled against Hudson's skin as he made the confession.

Hudson dropped his chin and sucked air as Cage kissed his neck. He was always instantly turned on by this man. It wasn't fair Cage had so much power over him. It had always been this way, even before any face-to-face meeting. Hudson could still remember the first time he caught himself flirting through the intercoms and the first time Cage's voice turned sultry. Nothing had changed. If anything, this connection between them grew stronger every day. Cage's parents thought Hudson was a miracle worker who saved their son. Hudson thought Cage was the miracle. Cage loved Hudson. No one understood Hudson was the one who had been saved in this scenario. In a matter of hours, under the stars and full moon, Hudson would gain a husband and parents. For the first time in years, he would have a real family. Cage had given him that. He wasn't scared of being twenty-one and married. After Cage, no one else could stack up.

Cage slid Hudson's zipper down. He moved slow, releasing it tooth by tooth as he sucked on Hudson's throat. "Come to bed with me. I don't want to wait until tonight to have you beneath me again."

Hudson couldn't deny him. He didn't want to say no. No matter what went on in other parts of the house, or how much company they had, Hudson was finally right where he wanted to be—locked away with his hero. He couldn't imagine a happier place existed anywhere in the world. Hudson would never try to find out.

Keep an eye out for the next Cubs for Rent, Second Choice.

Please consider leaving a review at the retailer where this book was purchased. Reviews really help with a book's visibility, which ensures I can continue writing. Thank you, Charity.

# ABOUT THE AUTHOR

Charity Parkerson is an award winning and multi-published author with several companies. Born with no filter from her brain to her mouth, she decided to take this odd quirk and insert it in her characters.

*Eight-time Readers' Favorite Award Winner
    *2015 Passionate Plume Award Finalist
    *2013 Reviewers' Choice Award Winner
    *2012 ARRA Finalist for Favorite Paranormal Romance
    *Five-time winner of The Mistress of the Darkpath

Connect with her online:

--Join          my          street          team: facebook.com/TeamCharityParkerson
    --Website: charityparkerson.com
    --Facebook: facebook.com/authorCharityParkerson

facebook.com/TheMenofSin

--Twitter: twitter.com/CharityParkerso

www.ingramcontent.com/pod-product-compliance
Lightning Source LLC
Chambersburg PA
CBHW060229180626
46813CB00007B/3012